ROAD TO THE KINGDOM

Twelve Women. One Journey. One Driver.

TARA A. GLOVER-JOHNSON

Published by:

Muse

Muse Technologies, Inc.
4601 Presidents Drive Suite 240
Lanham, MD 20706

Format	**ISBN**
Hardback	**979-8-951970-00-8**
Paperback	**979-8-951970-01-5**
Downloadable Audiobook	**979-8-951970-02-2**
Digital Online (eBook)	**979-8-951970-03-9**
Road to the Kingdom Journal (Paperback)	**979-8-951970-04-6**

Design by Spexalink Media Network

Dedication

For My Aunt Dot
Dorothy Brisbon

Every journey begins because someone believed we were worth walking beside.

Before I understood what it meant to be seen, chosen, or deeply loved, God placed someone in my life who quietly demonstrated all of those things. Her name is Dorothy Brisbon, but to me she has always been **Aunt Dot**.

Growing up in the '80s and '90s, there were seasons when the love, stability, and encouragement I desperately needed came through her. She was my safe place, my steady presence, and one of God's greatest gifts to my life.

I still remember the very first nightgown my Aunt Dot bought for me. I twirled and twirled until I was dizzy because, for the first time, I felt like a princess. Looking back now, I realize it was never really about the nightgown. It was about how she made me feel. She made me feel seen. She made me feel valued. She made me believe I mattered.

Aunt Dot loved me when I needed love. She encouraged me when I needed confidence; protected me when I needed safety; believed in me when I struggled to believe in myself.

As a teacher, she expected excellence from me. Not because perfection was the goal, but because she believed I was capable of becoming everything God created me to be. She filled my hands with books, knowing they would fill my mind with possibility. She challenged me to learn, to grow, and to dream beyond the circumstances around me.

More importantly, she took me to church. She didn't simply teach me about God; she introduced me to Him. Through her example of faith, kindness, humility, integrity, and unwavering work ethic, she helped lay the spiritual foundation upon which my life has been built. Looking back, I can see that foundation changed everything.

The women in this story each begin their journey carrying baggage shaped by rejection, shame, fear, comparison, disappointment, and longing. But none of us arrives where we are without someone God places along the way to remind us that we are seen, loved, and never truly alone. For me, that person was Aunt Dot.

Thank you for every prayer you prayed over me, every lesson you taught me, every book you placed in my hands, every ride to church, every word of encouragement, every act of protection, and every sacrifice you made that I may never fully know.

Your love helped shape the woman I became. This book exists, in part, because you were faithful to the calling God placed on your own life.

With all my love and deepest gratitude,

Tara

Contents

CHAPTER ONE
The Invitation—Hagar

Hagar unlocked the apartment door and stepped inside.

Silence greeted her. Not the peaceful kind. The heavy kind.

The kind that settled over a room after years of disappointment.

She dropped her purse onto the kitchen table and kicked off her shoes. Her feet throbbed from another twelve-hour shift at the assisted living facility. All day she cared for people who weren't her family. She had helped them eat, listened to their stories, comforted their fears, and held their hands through lonely moments.

Then she came home to an empty apartment. The irony was not lost on her.

For twenty years she had taken care of everyone else.

Her husband.

Her children.

Her parents.

Her church family.

Her clients.

Everyone.

Yet somehow, she had become the one nobody checked on.

She walked to the refrigerator and stared inside.

A bottle of water. Half a carton of eggs.

Leftovers she would probably throw away.

Closing the door, she sank into a chair and reached for her phone.

No missed calls. No text messages. Nothing.

Her thumb hovered over her daughter's contact information.

She considered calling.

Again. But she already knew how the conversation would go.

"Hi, baby."

"Hey, Mom. Can I call you back? I'm really busy right now."

Busy. Everyone was busy.

The word had become a polite replacement for goodbye.

Hagar laid the phone on the table and stared out the kitchen window.

Rain tapped softly against the glass.

Three years earlier her husband had walked out the front door and never returned.

Two years earlier her son had moved across the country.

One year earlier her daughter had stopped calling regularly.

And somewhere along the way, Hagar had begun believing a dangerous lie.

That she was forgettable.

A tear slid down her cheek before she could stop it.

She quickly wiped it away. There was no point crying. Nobody was there to see it.

The next morning began like every other.

Coffee.

Work.

Traffic.

More caregiving.

More smiling.

More pretending she was fine.

By the time she returned home that evening, darkness had settled across the city.

As she approached her apartment, something unusual caught her attention.

An envelope lay on the welcome mat.

She frowned.

Nobody mailed her letters anymore.

She picked it up.

No stamp. No return address. Just her name written in elegant gold lettering.

Hagar.

A strange chill ran through her.

Inside was a single cream-colored card.

Three words appeared in bold script.

BOARD THE BUS.

Beneath the message was another line.

Destination: The Kingdom.

Hagar laughed.

A short, nervous laugh.

"What kind of prank is this?"

She turned the card over.

Nothing. No explanation. No directions. No phone number.

No sender. Only those words.

She tossed it onto the kitchen table and walked away.

But hours later she found herself staring at it again.

The card seemed almost to glow beneath the lamp.

Not brightly. Just enough to draw her attention.

Something about it felt familiar.

Like a memory she couldn't quite reach.

Like a voice she hadn't heard in years.

That night, sleep came slowly.

And when it finally arrived, she dreamed.

She stood alone in a vast desert.

The sun burned overhead.

Heat shimmered across endless sand.

She was thirsty.

Exhausted. Afraid.

Then she noticed another woman nearby.

The woman looked strangely familiar.

She carried a child in her arms. Tears streaked her face.

She looked abandoned. Forgotten.

The woman collapsed beneath a small tree.

Hagar's heart broke for her.

Then a voice echoed across the desert.

Strong. Gentle. Powerful.

"Hagar."

The woman lifted her head.

Not me, Hagar thought.

Her. The other woman.

The voice spoke again.

"I see you."

Suddenly water burst from the ground.

A spring emerged where moments before there had been nothing but dry earth.

Life where death had seemed certain.

Hope where despair had ruled.

Hagar woke with tears on her cheeks.

The dream felt real.

More real than her apartment.

More real than the rain tapping against the windows.

She sat up in bed and looked toward the kitchen.

The invitation still rested on the table.

Waiting.

Three days later she found herself standing at an address she did not remember looking up.

A bus station.

The sky above was brilliant blue.

Dozens of women stood nearby holding identical invitations.

Some appeared nervous.

Others excited.

A few looked as confused as she felt.

At the center of the lot stood the most beautiful bus Hagar had ever seen.

Its polished exterior reflected sunlight like gold.

The destination sign above the windshield glowed softly.

THE KINGDOM.

Hagar clutched her purse tighter.

Every instinct told her to leave.

This was ridiculous.

Impossible. Crazy.

Yet something deeper urged her forward.

A sense that her entire life had been leading to this moment.

The bus doors opened.

A warm voice called out.

"Welcome, daughters."

The women began boarding.

One by one.

Hagar remained frozen.

The voice spoke again.

Not loudly.

Not forcefully.

Simply with love.

"We've been expecting you."

Something inside her broke.

Not painfully. Beautifully.

For years she had believed nobody was waiting for her.

Nobody was looking for her.

Nobody noticed whether she arrived or not.

Yet somehow the voice carried the certainty of truth.

She was expected. Wanted. Known.

Hagar wiped her eyes and stepped forward.

As her foot touched the first step of the bus, she paused.

The scent of something warm and familiar drifted from inside.

Not perfume. Not air freshener. Something deeper.

Something that reminded her of her grandmother's kitchen on Sunday mornings.

Of safety. Of belonging. Of home.

Soft voices murmured from within.

The sound of women settling into seats.

The gentle creak of the bus as it breathed and waited.

And underneath it all, a quiet melody she almost recognized.

Something ancient. Something tender.

Something that sounded like her name being sung rather than spoken.

She exhaled slowly. Then stepped inside.

She glanced back once at the life she was leaving behind.

The loneliness. The rejection. The endless striving.

Then she turned toward the open doorway.

Toward the journey. Toward the Kingdom.

And toward the Driver who had seen her all along.

CHAPTER TWO

The Invitation—Rebekah

Rebekah checked her phone for the third time in ten minutes.

Nothing.

No text.

No missed call.

No update.

She set the phone on the kitchen counter and immediately picked it back up.

Still nothing.

Outside her window, autumn leaves drifted across the lawn of the house she had lived in for nearly thirty years. Everything appeared calm.

Inside, however, was another story.

Rebekah's mind was a storm.

She walked into the dining room and straightened a stack of mail that was already perfectly aligned.

Then she adjusted the chair.

Then she wiped an invisible smudge from the table.

Then she glanced at her phone again.

Nothing. The silence felt unbearable.

Three months earlier, her son Daniel had called with news she never expected.

"Mom, I'm moving." The words had hit her like a punch.

"Moving where?"

"Seattle."

"Seattle?" she repeated. "When did this happen?"

"I accepted the position a few weeks ago."

A few weeks.

The phrase still stung.

Not because he was moving.

Because he had decided without her.

Without asking her opinion.

Without seeking her advice. Without needing her.

For fifty-eight years, Rebekah had been the woman everyone depended on.

The organizer. The problem-solver. The planner. The fixer.

If something went wrong, people called Rebekah.

If a family crisis erupted, Rebekah handled it.

If someone needed answers, Rebekah found them.

She carried calendars, lists, schedules, and contingency plans as though they were life preservers.

Control made her feel safe. Necessary. Valuable.

Now Daniel was building a life that no longer revolved around her guidance.

The realization terrified her more than she wanted to admit.

Her phone buzzed suddenly. Rebekah grabbed it.

A sales notification. She sighed heavily.

"Lord, I don't know what You're doing."

The words escaped before she realized she had spoken them aloud.

The room fell silent.

For the first time in a long while, she allowed herself to ask the question she had been avoiding.

What happens when people no longer need me?

The thought unsettled her.

She walked to the window.

A memory surfaced.

Daniel taking his first steps.

Daniel graduating high school.

Daniel leaving for college.

Daniel becoming a man.

Every season of his life had required her a little less.

And perhaps that was how it was supposed to be.

Yet letting go felt impossible.

That evening, a storm rolled through the city.

Rain hammered against the windows.

Thunder rumbled overhead.

When Rebekah heard a knock at the door, she frowned.

No one visited unannounced.

Especially not during a storm.

She opened the door. No one stood outside.

Only an envelope resting neatly on the welcome mat.

Her name was written across the front in elegant gold lettering.

Rebekah.

She looked around.

The street was empty.

The rain continued to fall.

Slowly she picked up the envelope and carried it inside.

There was no stamp. No return address.

No indication of who had sent it.

Inside was a single card.

Simple. Cream colored. Beautiful.

Three words appeared in bold script.

BOARD THE BUS.

Below it were four smaller words.

Destination: The Kingdom.

Rebekah stared.

Then laughed.

"Well, that's certainly different."

She flipped the card over.

Nothing.

No instructions.

No explanation.

No contact information.

Only the invitation.

She set it on the counter and returned to her evening routine.

Yet throughout the night she found herself glancing at it.

Again.

And again.

Something about the card unsettled her.

Not in a frightening way.

In a familiar way.

As if someone who knew her completely had written it.

When she finally fell asleep, she dreamed.

She stood in a vast desert beneath a sky filled with stars.

A young woman approached carrying a water jar.

The woman was beautiful.

Confident.

Purposeful.

She knelt beside a well.

Servants waited nearby.

Camels drank from stone troughs.

Rebekah recognized the story immediately.

The biblical Rebekah.

Chosen.

Called.

Blessed.

The scene shifted.

Years passed.

Now the woman paced anxiously inside a tent.

Worry filled her eyes.

Fear.

Doubt.

Urgency.

God had made a promise.

Yet she no longer trusted Him to fulfill it.

So, she took matters into her own hands.

A plan. A deception. A shortcut.

The dream ended with a family divided.

A son running away.

A mother left behind.

The image lingered long after Rebekah awoke.

For days she could not shake it.

Every time she looked at the invitation, the dream returned.

Every time she thought about Daniel, the dream returned.

Every time she tried to plan her future, the dream returned.

Finally, three days later, she found herself standing in front of an unfamiliar bus station.

The invitation rested in her hand.

Women gathered nearby.

Some looked nervous.

Others appeared excited.

Several seemed just as confused as she felt.

Then she saw it.

The bus.

Its polished exterior gleamed beneath the morning sun.

The destination sign above the windshield glowed softly.

THE KINGDOM.

Rebekah's heart raced.

This was absurd.

Completely absurd.

She should leave.

Go home.

Create a plan.

Research the situation.

Gather information.

Ask questions.

Instead, she stood frozen.

The bus doors opened.

A warm voice echoed from within.

"Welcome, daughters."

One by one, the women began boarding.

Rebekah remained where she was.

The Driver appeared in the doorway.

Though she could not fully explain it, His presence felt familiar.

Like a voice she had heard her entire life.

Patient.

Steady.

Certain.

As though He already knew every fear she carried.

Their eyes met.

The Driver smiled.

"We've been expecting you, Rebekah."

Something inside her shifted.

Not dramatically. Not all at once. Just enough.

Enough to loosen her grip on certainty.

Enough to take one step forward.

Then another.

And another.

As she climbed the steps of the bus, she noticed a leather planner tucked beneath her arm.

She hadn't realized she was carrying it.

Inside were schedules.

Lists.

Budgets.

Goals.

Backup plans.

Emergency plans.

Plans for plans.

The Driver glanced at it knowingly.

Rebekah held it tighter.

Not yet.

She wasn't ready to let it go.

She found an empty seat near the front.

Of course, near the front.

Where she could observe everything.

Track every turn.

Anticipate every stop.

A woman was already seated across the aisle.

She had warm brown eyes and the quiet look of someone who had been carrying something heavy for a very long time.

She glanced up and offered a small smile.

"I almost didn't come," the woman said softly.

Rebekah straightened in her seat.

"Neither did I."

A brief silence settled between them.

Not uncomfortable.

Just honest.

"I'm Hagar," the woman said.

"Rebekah."

They nodded at each other the way women do when they recognize something familiar in a stranger.

Something unspoken.

Something understood.

The bus doors closed behind them.

The engine rumbled to life.

And somewhere deep within her soul, a lesson had already begun.

Faith did not require understanding every detail.

Faith required getting on the bus.

CHAPTER THREE
The Invitation—Lot's Wife

Lot's Wife kept the box on the top shelf of her closet.

She told herself she should throw it away.

She never did.

For ten years the box had followed her from house to house.

Apartment to apartment.

Storage unit to storage unit.

Always packed. Always protected. Always waiting.

Tonight, like so many nights before, she pulled it down and carried it to the kitchen table.

The cardboard corners were worn now.

The tape had yellowed with age.

Slowly she opened the lid.

Inside were pieces of another life.

Photographs. Award plaques. Old birthday cards.

A wedding album. A newspaper clipping announcing her promotion.

A key to a house she no longer owned.

A life she no longer lived.

She picked up a photograph.

There she was. Smiling. Successful. Confident.

The woman in the picture seemed like a stranger now.

Back then she had everything.

A thriving real estate business.

A beautiful home.

A husband she believed would love her forever.

Friends.

Status.

Security.

Then life happened.

The economy crashed.

The business failed.

The marriage ended.

The house was sold.

One loss after another until the woman in the photograph disappeared.

Yet Lot's Wife couldn't let her go.

Every night she revisited those memories.

Every night she compared her present to her past.

And every night she felt the same ache.

Life was better then.

At least that's what she told herself.

The truth was more complicated.

But memory has a way of editing pain and preserving only what it wants us to see.

Her phone buzzed. She glanced down. A social media notification.

Another former colleague celebrating another success.

Another smiling family. Another dream fulfilled.

Lot's Wife sighed and set the phone aside.

The room suddenly felt smaller. Lonelier.

The silence pressed against her chest like a stone.

She looked around the modest apartment she now called home.

Everything felt temporary.

Nothing felt like hers.

The thought came again.

The same thought she wrestled with nearly every day.

If only things could go back to the way they were.

Outside, rain had begun.

Not gently. In sheets.

Lightning cracked across the dark sky.

Thunder followed seconds later.

She rose to close the curtains.

That's when she saw it.

An envelope resting on the floor just inside her front door.

Her heart skipped.

She hadn't heard anyone knock.

No mail slot existed in the door.

No one had entered.

Yet there it was.

Waiting.

She approached cautiously.

Her name appeared across the front in elegant gold lettering.

Lot's Wife.

The sight startled her.

Not her legal name.

Not the name on her driver's license.

The name she carried in secret.

The name that haunted her.

The woman who looked back.

The woman who couldn't let go.

With trembling fingers, she opened the envelope.

Inside was a cream-colored card.

Simple.

Beautiful.

Three words appeared in bold script.

BOARD THE BUS.

Below it:

Destination: The Kingdom.

Lot's Wife frowned.

"What kind of invitation is this?"

She turned it over.

Nothing.

No address.

No sender.

No explanation.

Just the invitation.

She almost threw it away.

Almost.

Instead, she left it on the kitchen counter.

For the next three days it followed her everywhere.

Not physically. Mentally.

The card lingered in her thoughts.

At work. At home. While driving.

While trying to sleep.

Especially while trying to sleep.

On the third night she dreamed.

She stood on a road beneath a blood-red sky.

Smoke rose in the distance.

The air smelled of fire and ash.

Ahead of her walked a family.

A man. Two daughters. And a woman.

The woman looked familiar.

Painfully familiar.

The woman was crying.

Not because she feared the future.

Because she couldn't release the past.

A voice echoed from heaven.

Strong.

Certain.

Merciful.

"Do not look back."

The family continued forward.

The woman hesitated.

One final glance.

One final longing look.

One final attachment.

Then everything froze.

The dream shattered.

Lot's Wife woke gasping.

Her heart pounded violently.

The room was dark and still.

The invitation sat on the nightstand.

Waiting.

She stared at it for a long time.

Then she thought of Hagar.

The woman who had been cast out with nothing.

Who had sat in the desert believing she was forgotten.

Yet God had seen her.

Had spoken to her.

Had provided water where there was only sand.

She thought of Rebekah.

The woman who had tried to control every outcome.

Who had gripped her plans so tightly she couldn't feel God's hand.

Yet God had called her forward anyway.

What if the invitation wasn't just for them?

What if it was for her too?

By morning she had made a decision.

She didn't understand the invitation.

She didn't understand the destination.

But she knew one thing.

She couldn't keep living in yesterday.

Three days later she stood at a bus station unlike any she had ever seen.

Women gathered nearby holding identical invitations.

Some smiled nervously.

Others looked excited.

A few appeared afraid.

Lot's Wife recognized something familiar in their faces.

They were all carrying something.

Not luggage.

Burdens.

The kind people carry inside.

She noticed two women already seated near the front of the bus through the large windows.

One woman with warm brown eyes who seemed to be exhaling for the first time in years.

The other one with a leather planner resting firmly in her lap.

Something about seeing them there steadied her.

They had come too.

They had chosen the bus.

Then she saw the destination sign above the windshield glowing softly in the morning light.

THE KINGDOM.

Her breath caught.

A strange peace settled over the station.

The bus doors opened.

A warm voice called out.

"Welcome, daughters."

The women began boarding.

One by one.

Lot's Wife remained still.

Fear rooted her to the ground.

Not fear of the bus.

Fear of moving forward.

Fear of what she might have to leave behind.

The Driver appeared in the doorway.

His eyes met hers.

Not judgmental.

Not impatient.

Knowing.

As though He had witnessed every night she sat alone with her memories.

Every tear.

Every regret.

Every longing.

The Driver smiled.

"We've been expecting you."

Tears filled her eyes.

No one had said those words to her in years.

Expected.

Wanted.

Welcomed.

The box.

The photographs.

The old life.

The memories.

She thought of all of it.

Then she looked at the bus.

At the open door.

At the Driver.

For the first time, she wondered if there might be something better ahead than what she kept looking back toward.

Slowly she stepped forward.

One step.

Then another.

And another.

As she climbed the stairs, she noticed something in her hands.

The box.

The same worn cardboard box she had carried for years.

The Driver glanced toward it.

His smile remained gentle.

Lot's Wife tightened her grip.

Not yet.

She wasn't ready to let it go.

But she boarded anyway.

As she moved down the aisle, she passed the woman with warm brown eyes.

Hagar looked up.

Their eyes met briefly.

No words were exchanged.

None were needed.

Just the quiet recognition of two women who understood what it meant to carry something too heavy for too long.

Lot's Wife found a seat and settled in.

The doors closed behind her.

The engine came to life.

And somewhere deep within her heart, a battle had already begun.

The battle between yesterday and tomorrow.

Between memory and promise.

Between looking back and moving forward.

The road to the Kingdom stretched ahead.

And for the first time in a very long time, Lot's Wife faced the future.

CHAPTER FOUR
The Invitation—Leah

Leah had learned early that some people are seen and some people are overlooked.

She had a sister named Rachel.

That was where the lesson began.

Not in a single moment, but slowly, over years of standing in the same room and watching the air change when Rachel walked in.

The way conversations shifted.

The way eyes moved.

The way laughter rose a little higher.

The way ordinary rooms became beautiful simply because Rachel had entered them.

It was not Rachel's fault.

That was the part that made it hardest to carry.

Rachel did not try to outshine her. Rachel simply was bright and beautiful and magnetic in the way some people are born, without effort or apology.

And Leah—faithful, steady, tender-eyed Leah—had learned to make herself smaller so the contrast would not hurt as much.

It hurt anyway.

They had grown up in the same house. Eaten at the same table. Been daughters of the same father.

And still, somehow, Leah had always felt slightly outside the frame of her own life.

Present.

But not quite pictured.

There.

But not quite seen.

She loved Rachel.

Genuinely.

Completely.

In the complicated way you love someone who has everything you quietly ache for, not because you wish it taken from them, but because you wonder in the small hours of the night why it was never offered to you.

Leah had been given to Jacob first.

She had not chosen it.

Her father had arranged it, had covered her face and sent her in the dark to a man who was waiting for someone else.

And Jacob, when morning came and the veil was lifted, had looked at her with an expression she had never been able to forget.

Disappointment.

Not cruelty.

Not hatred.

Just the quiet, devastating recognition that she was not who he had been hoping for.

He had worked seven more years for Rachel.

Seven years.

And Leah had spent those years being faithful to a man whose heart lived somewhere else. Cooking his meals, keeping his home, bearing his children, hoping that each son would be the thing that finally made him turn toward her and stay.

Reuben.

Surely now my husband will love me.

Simeon.

Because the Lord heard I was unloved.

Levi.

Now at last my husband will be attached to me.

Judah.

This time I will praise the Lord.

Four sons.

Four prayers wrapped in names.

Four times she placed her hope in something that did not fill the hollow place.

Eventually, she stopped naming children after her longing.

But the longing itself had never fully stopped.

Now, in another life and another time, Leah followed Rachel on social media.

She did not announce it.

She simply watched the way Leah had always watched Rachel—from a careful, quiet distance that looked like contentment if no one looked too closely.

Rachel's page was everything Leah expected it to be.

Beautiful.

Curated.

Full of golden light, laughing children, and a husband who still looked at her the way Jacob always had, as if she were the answer to a question he had been asking his whole life.

Leah scrolled slowly.

She did not begrudge her sister the life.

She had made her peace with that.

Or something close enough to peace that she had stopped examining the difference.

Then she saw the post.

Rachel had posted their anniversary photo on a Tuesday afternoon. Leah saw it while folding laundry, her phone propped against the basket, the notification appearing at the top of the screen like a small, quiet summons.

She set down the shirt she was folding and picked up the phone.

The photo was stunning.

Of course it was.

Rachel stood in golden light, her husband's arm around her, the children laughing in the background like joy was the only language they had ever been taught.

The caption read:

Five years of chosen. Five years of love. Five years of grateful. #Blessed #StillMyPerson #FamilyFirst #GratefulHeart

Leah read it once.

Then she read it again.

Five years of chosen.

She sat with that for a long moment.

The laundry basket at her feet.

The afternoon light coming through the window at an angle that made everything look softer than it was.

She thought about what it felt like to be chosen.

To be the one someone ran toward instead of settled for.

To post a photo and know, really know, that the man standing beside you had chosen you first, chosen you freely, chosen you without arrangement or obligation or the cover of darkness.

She thought about Jacob's face on that first morning.

She put the phone down.

Then picked it up again.

Her thumb hovered over the screen.

For a moment, she wanted to do nothing.

Not out of bitterness.

Out of exhaustion.

There were only so many times a heart could smile at the thing that reminded it of its wound.

Then Leah inhaled slowly.

And pressed "like."

Not because it was easy.

Not because the ache had stopped.

But because love—real love, the kind that costs something—sometimes looks like pressing like on a photo that takes something from you.

She set the phone face down on top of the folded laundry and returned to her work.

She did not leave a comment.

She did not send a message.

She simply did what she had always done.

Showed up quietly.

Faithfully.

Without fanfare.

For a sister who had not noticed she was there.

The invitation arrived three days later.

Leah almost missed it.

It was tucked between a water bill and a church bulletin she had been meaning to read; a small cream-colored envelope with her name written across the front in handwriting that felt like a voice she recognized from somewhere deep and old.

She stood at the kitchen counter and opened it slowly.

Inside was a single card.

Simple.

Cream-colored.

Beautiful.

Three words appeared in bold script.

BOARD THE BUS.

Below it:

Destination: The Kingdom.

Leah stared.

She turned it over.

Nothing.

No address.

No sender.

No explanation.

Just the invitation.

She almost threw it away.

Almost.

Instead, she set it on the kitchen counter and returned to her evening routine.

But throughout the night, she found herself glancing at it.

Again.

And again.

Something about the card unsettled her.

Not in a frightening way.

In a familiar way.

As if someone who knew her completely had written it.

As if the handwriting belonged to someone who had been watching for a very long time and had finally decided to speak.

When she fell asleep that night, she dreamed.

She stood inside a tent at the edge of a vast plain.

The air smelled of fire and bread and the particular dust of a place where people lived close to the ground.

Outside, she could hear the sounds of a camp settling into evening, children quieting, fires crackling, and the low murmur of men's voices.

Inside the tent, a woman sat alone.

She was not beautiful in the way that made people stop.

She was beautiful in the way that takes longer to see. Steady eyes, capable hands, a face that had learned to hold still even when everything inside was moving.

Leah recognized her immediately.

She was watching herself.

The woman folded clothes.

Working quietly.

Faithfully.

Without announcement.

Without audience.

Without the urgency of someone who needed to be noticed doing the thing.

Then the tent flap opened.

A man entered.

He looked at the woman briefly.

Not unkindly.

But not with the look that fills a hollow place.

He looked at her the way one looks at something reliable. A table, a chair, something that will be there when needed and will not require attention when not.

Then he looked past her toward the entrance of the tent, as though waiting for someone else.

The woman continued folding.

She did not stop.

She did not look up.

But Leah, watching from the edge of the dream, saw what the woman's face did when the man looked past her.

She had seen that expression in mirrors.

The dream shifted.

Now the woman sat in the dark with a sleeping child in her arms.

She was not weeping.

She was past the kind of weeping that makes sound.

She was doing the other kind.

The quiet kind.

The kind that happens in the middle of the night when everyone else is asleep and there is no one to perform composure for.

Then a voice filled the dream.

Not loud.

Not dramatic.

Not thunder or wind.

Just present.

Close.

The way a voice sounds when it is speaking directly to you and no one else.

"The Lord has seen your affliction."

The woman looked up.

The child stirred.

The voice continued.

"You have not been overlooked. You have not been forgotten. The one who is unseen by men is fully seen by Me."

The woman closed her eyes.

Something moved across her face that Leah had not seen there before.

Not happiness.

Not resolution.

Something quieter.

Relief.

The relief of someone who has been carrying a question for a very long time and has finally been given an answer. Not the answer that changes the circumstances, but the answer that changes what the circumstances mean.

The dream ended.

Leah woke in the early hours of morning.

The room was dark and still.

The invitation sat on the nightstand.

Waiting.

She stared at it for a long time.

Then she thought of Hagar, the woman who had been cast into the wilderness with nothing. The woman who sat beneath a burning sky believing she was forgotten, yet God had seen her, spoken to her by name, provided water where there was only sand.

She thought of Rebekah, the woman who tried to control every outcome and still found herself being called forward.

She thought of Lot's Wife, the woman who could not stop looking back.

What if the invitation was not only for women with grand stories?

What if it was for women like her?

Quiet women.

Faithful women.

Women who pressed "like" on Tuesday afternoons and put the phone face down on top of the laundry.

By morning, she had made a decision.

She did not fully understand the invitation.

She did not understand the destination.

But she understood the handwriting.

She understood the name written across the front of the envelope. Not a title, not a role, not wife of Jacob or mother of sons or sister of Rachel.

Just her name.

Plain.

Complete.

Enough on its own.

Leah.

She packed a bag that evening.

She folded two changes of clothes. She tucked in her worn Bible, the one with highlighted verses and notes in the margins, the one that fell open automatically to Genesis 29 because she had read it so many times the spine had memorized the place.

She paused before closing the bag.

Then she reached for the invitation and tucked it beside the Bible.

She did not know where she was going.

But she had learned slowly, over years of faithfulness in the dark, that you do not always need to understand the destination to trust the One calling you toward it.

Three days after the invitation arrived, Leah stood at a bus station unlike any she had ever seen.

Women gathered nearby, each holding an identical cream-colored invitation. Some smiled nervously. Others looked excited. A few appeared afraid.

Leah recognized something familiar in their faces. The particular expression of women who had been carrying something for a long time and were not yet certain they were allowed to set it down.

Then she noticed the bus.

It was quieter than she expected.

More ordinary.

She had imagined something that matched the weight of the moment, something that announced itself. Instead, it sat steady and waiting in the early morning light, unhurried, as though it had all the time in the world and had been expecting her specifically.

The destination sign above the windshield glowed softly.

THE KINGDOM.

Her breath caught.

The bus doors opened.

A warm voice called from within.

"Welcome, daughters."

The women began boarding.

One by one.

Leah remained still.

Not because she had decided against it.

Because something in her wanted to stand there for just one more moment. To feel the weight of what it meant to be called, to be expected, to be invited somewhere by name.

The Driver appeared in the doorway.

He looked at her without surprise.

His eyes held something she had not seen directed at her in a very long time.

Not pity.

Not patience wearing the face of kindness.

Not the particular look of someone making room because they had to.

Recognition.

As though He had been watching for her specifically.

As though her arrival was not a pleasant surprise but a long-anticipated certainty.

"Leah," He said.

Just her name.

Nothing added.

Nothing qualified.

Not Leah the overlooked.

Not Leah the unloved.

Not Leah who was not the one he wanted.

Just Leah.

Complete.

Whole.

Enough on its own.

"I'm expected?" she asked.

Her voice was quieter than she intended.

The Driver smiled.

"You have always been expected. I have been waiting for you specifically."

Tears filled her eyes.

Expected.

Wanted.

Welcomed.

She thought of the labels she had carried.

Not Pretty Enough.

Second Choice.

Invisible.

Unwanted.

She thought of Jacob's face on that first morning.

She thought of four sons named after a longing that never fully quieted.

She thought of a Tuesday afternoon and a phone set face down on top of laundry.

Then she looked at the bus.

At the open door.

At the Driver.

And she stepped forward.

One step.

Then another.

And another.

As she climbed the stairs, she noticed the worn leather bag hanging from her shoulder, its surface covered with labels rubbed smooth by years of handling.

She had carried it so long she had stopped noticing its weight.

The Driver glanced toward it.

His smile remained gentle.

Leah tightened her grip.

Not yet.

She was not ready to let it go.

But she boarded anyway.

Leah found a seat near the window and settled into it the way she settled into most things without drama, without announcement, simply present.

She placed her worn leather bag at her feet.

Only now did she notice the faded labels stitched across the bag's surface.

Invisible.

Second Choice.

Not Enough.

The words looked as though they had been there for years.

Perhaps they had.

She reached down and ran her fingers across one of them.

The Driver walked slowly down the aisle, welcoming each passenger with the same quiet kindness.

When He reached Leah's seat, His eyes rested briefly on the bag.

He smiled.

"You've carried that a long time."

Leah instinctively slipped her foot in front of it.

"It belongs to me."

"For now," He replied gently.

She looked up.

"What does that mean?"

The Driver's smile deepened.

"You'll understand before the journey ends."

Then He continued down the aisle.

Leah watched Him greet the other women as they boarded.

Each one looked different.

Different ages.

Different backgrounds.

Different expressions.

Yet each carried a bag.

Some were elegant.

Some worn.

Some overflowing.

One woman clutched hers as though someone might steal it.

Another kept looking over her shoulder before stepping onto the bus.

Leah wondered what stories they carried.

She wondered if their bags felt as heavy as hers.

Outside, more women were arriving.

One by one.

No one spoke much.

It felt as though they all understood this was no ordinary journey.

Leah rested her hand on the window.

The morning light stretched across the empty platform.

Someone else was coming.

She didn't know why she felt so certain.

She simply did.

The Driver returned to the front of the bus.

He looked out through the windshield, almost as though He, too, was waiting.

Waiting for every daughter who had received an invitation.

Leah leaned back in her seat.

For the first time in years, she felt no pressure to become someone else.

She didn't have to earn her place.

She had been invited.

She was expected.

She was enough.

The engine started with a quiet hum.

But the bus did not move.

Not yet.

It was still waiting.

Just as the Driver was.

Just as, perhaps, Heaven had always been.

Leah glanced once more at the platform outside.

Somewhere beyond the station, another invitation was being opened.

Another heart was beginning to awaken.

Another story was about to begin.

She didn't know her name.

Not yet.

But before this journey was over…

their stories would become one.

The Driver closed the door with a gentle smile.

"Welcome," He said softly.

"The journey is just beginning."

CHAPTER FIVE

The Invitation—Abigail

Abigail's phone rang before her feet touched the floor.

She glanced at the clock.

4:57 a.m.

Too early for good news.

With a sigh, she reached for the phone on the nightstand.

"Hello?"

"Abigail, I'm sorry to call so early."

The voice belonged to a member of her church.

Immediately Abigail sat up.

"What's wrong?"

For the next twenty minutes she listened.

A family crisis.

A marriage in trouble.

A daughter who had run away.

Fear.

Tears.

Questions.

The same kind of call she had answered hundreds of times before.

When the conversation finally ended, Abigail prayed with the woman, offered encouragement, and promised to follow up later.

By the time she hung up, sleep was gone.

So was the possibility of rest.

She rose from bed and quietly made her way to the kitchen.

Outside, darkness still covered the city.

Inside, the coffee maker hummed to life.

Abigail leaned against the counter and rubbed her tired eyes.

Fifty-two years old.

Executive pastor.

Counselor.

Teacher.

Mentor.

Problem-solver.

Peacemaker.

The titles never ended.

Neither did the needs.

Everyone came to Abigail.

People sought her wisdom.

Trusted her judgment.

Leaned on her strength.

Yet very few people ever asked a simple question.

How are you?

The answer would have surprised them.

Exhausted.

Lonely.

Running on fumes.

Abigail wrapped her hands around a coffee mug and stared out the window.

The city was waking up slowly.

Headlights moved along distant streets.

A delivery truck idled at the corner.

Somewhere out there, people were beginning their days.

She was already ending hers.

She couldn't remember the last time she had done something for herself.

Even her prayers often focused on everyone else's problems.

Everyone else's healing.

Everyone else's breakthrough.

Everyone else's pain.

Somewhere along the way she had become responsible for carrying burdens that weren't hers.

Her phone buzzed again.

A text message.

Then another.

Meeting requests.

Counseling appointments.

Volunteer issues.

Schedule changes.

Questions.

Needs.

Demands.

Abigail closed her eyes.

For just a moment, she wished everyone would stop needing her.

The thought immediately filled her with guilt.

Good women didn't think things like that.

At least that's what she had always told herself.

The rest of the day unfolded exactly as expected.

Meetings.

Phone calls.

Encouragement.

Conflict resolution.

More meetings.

More phone calls.

More encouragement.

By the time she finally arrived home, darkness had returned.

Her shoulders ached.

Her head throbbed.

Her soul felt empty.

The house greeted her with silence.

She should have appreciated the quiet.

Instead, it felt unfamiliar.

She had become so accustomed to solving everyone else's problems that she no longer knew what to do when no one needed her.

Abigail dropped her bag onto the dining room chair.

As she turned toward the kitchen, something caught her attention.

An envelope rested on the table.

She frowned.

She hadn't left it there.

Carefully she picked it up.

Her name was written across the front in elegant gold lettering.

Abigail.

The sight stirred something deep within her.

A memory.

A woman from Scripture.

Wise.

Courageous.

A peacemaker.

A woman who stepped between destruction and salvation.

A woman who carried responsibility for everyone around her.

She had always admired that woman.

She had never considered how exhausted that woman must have been.

Slowly she opened the envelope.

Inside was a cream-colored card.

Simple.

Beautiful.

Three words appeared in bold script.

BOARD THE BUS.

Below them:

Destination: The Kingdom.

Abigail stared.

"What bus?"

She turned the card over.

Nothing.

No address.

No instructions.

No explanation.

Only the invitation.

For some reason, tears filled her eyes.

Not because she understood it.

Because she didn't.

For once there was no problem to solve.

No strategy to create.

No plan to manage.

Only an invitation.

Just for her.

She thought of the other women who must have received the same card.

Women who had been cast out.

Women who had tried to control everything.

Women who couldn't stop looking backward.

Women who had spent their lives invisible.

Each of them had been called.

And so had she.

That night she fell asleep almost immediately.

And dreamed.

She stood on a dusty road beneath a blazing sun.

Ahead, a woman raced toward a group of armed men.

Fear gripped Abigail's chest.

The woman should have been terrified.

Instead, she moved with confidence.

Purpose.

Wisdom.

Abigail recognized her instantly.

The biblical Abigail.

The woman who intervened between David and disaster.

The woman who prevented bloodshed.

The woman who saved an entire household.

The scene shifted.

Again, Abigail watched the woman solving problems.

Protecting people.

Preventing conflict.

Carrying responsibility.

Fixing situations nobody else could fix.

Then suddenly everything changed.

The woman stopped.

For the first time, she laid down what she was carrying.

The burden.

The responsibility.

The need to save everyone.

The moment felt strange.

Unnatural.

Yet peaceful.

A voice echoed through the dream.

"You were never meant to carry them all."

Abigail woke suddenly.

Her heart raced.

The room was dark.

The invitation sat on her nightstand.

Waiting.

The words from the dream lingered.

You were never meant to carry them all.

For three days she couldn't stop thinking about them.

Every counseling session.

Every meeting.

Every crisis.

The phrase followed her.

By the fourth morning, she found herself standing at an unfamiliar bus station.

Women gathered nearby holding invitations identical to hers.

Some looked nervous.

Others excited.

Many appeared wounded.

Broken.

Searching.

Abigail noticed something else.

Every woman carried baggage.

Some visible.

Some hidden.

Through the large windows of the bus, she could see women already seated inside.

The one with warm brown eyes seemed to be breathing easier than she had in years.

One was gripping a leather planner with both hands.

One was clutching a worn cardboard box against her chest.

One had a heavy leather bag draped over her shoulder, covered in small paper tags.

Each of them had answered the call.

Each of them had come.

And none of them looked like they had it all together.

The realization was strangely comforting.

Then she saw the bus.

Its polished exterior reflected the morning sunlight.

Above the windshield glowed a destination sign.

THE KINGDOM.

A strange peace settled over her.

For the first time in years, she wasn't responsible for organizing anything.

She wasn't leading.

Planning.

Teaching.

Fixing.

She was simply a passenger.

The thought felt both comforting and terrifying.

The bus doors opened.

A warm voice called out.

"Welcome, daughters."

One by one, the women began boarding.

Abigail waited near the back.

Old habits died hard.

Others first.

Always others first.

As she stood there, she noticed something slung across her shoulder.

A large leather satchel.

Much heavier than she remembered.

When she opened it, she gasped.

Inside were burdens.

Not physical objects.

People's burdens.

Worries.

Heartaches.

Failures.

Disappointments.

Responsibilities.

Names.

Hundreds of names.

People she had spent years trying to rescue.

Years trying to carry.

Years trying to fix.

The weight nearly brought her to tears.

The Driver appeared in the doorway.

His eyes rested briefly on the satchel.

Then on her.

Compassion filled His expression.

Not judgment.

Not disappointment.

Compassion.

"We've been expecting you, Abigail."

The words pierced her heart.

Not because someone needed her.

Because someone *wanted* her.

Abigail tightened her grip on the satchel.

She wasn't ready to put it down.

Not yet.

But she stepped forward.

One step.

Then another.

As she crossed the threshold of the bus, a small part of the burden seemed lighter.

Not gone.

Just lighter.

She moved down the aisle slowly.

As she passed each woman, something passed between them.

A glance.

A nod.

A quiet recognition.

You too.

Yes. Me too.

She found an empty seat and settled in.

For the first time in decades, Abigail boarded a journey where she wasn't responsible for everyone else.

The doors closed behind her.

The engine rumbled to life.

And deep within her heart, a lesson had already begun.

The Savior had never asked her to become one.

The road stretched ahead.

And Abigail's journey toward rest had finally begun.

CHAPTER SIX

The Invitation—Bathsheba

Bathsheba stood alone in the conference room long after everyone else had left.

The city skyline stretched beyond the floor-to-ceiling windows, glittering beneath the evening sky.

Thousands of lights illuminated the darkness below.

Most people would have called it a beautiful view.

Bathsheba barely noticed.

She stared at her reflection in the glass.

Polished.

Professional.

Successful.

The image looking back at her had taken years to build.

Years of hard work.

Years of proving herself.

Years of carefully reconstructing a life that had nearly collapsed.

The promotion announcement still sat on the conference table.

Senior Vice President.

A title many people spent their entire careers chasing.

Her colleagues had celebrated.

There had been speeches.

Champagne.

Applause.

Smiles.

Yet even now, standing alone, Bathsheba felt none of the joy she was supposed to feel.

Instead, she felt the familiar whisper.

The same whisper that had followed her for years.

If they knew everything, they wouldn't be celebrating you.

She closed her eyes.

The memory surfaced immediately.

A headline.

A scandal.

A mistake that became public.

Photographs.

Rumors.

Judgment.

Endless conversations happening in rooms she couldn't enter.

Years had passed since then.

Most people had forgotten.

Bathsheba hadn't.

She carried it everywhere.

The shame.

The regret.

The humiliation.

Some wounds heal.

Others simply become easier to hide.

Her phone vibrated.

A text from a colleague.

Congratulations again. You deserve this.

Bathsheba stared at the words.

Deserve.

The word made her uncomfortable.

She wasn't sure she deserved any of it.

Not after everything.

She slipped the phone into her purse and headed toward the elevator.

The office building was nearly empty.

Only a few employees remained.

The elevator doors opened.

She stepped inside.

As the doors closed, she caught her reflection once more.

For a brief moment, she saw something else.

Not the successful executive.

Not the accomplished professional.

A frightened woman desperately trying to outrun her past.

The image disappeared as quickly as it came.

By the time she reached the lobby, the feeling remained.

The drive home was quiet.

Rain tapped softly against the windshield.

The radio played in the background, but she barely listened.

Her thoughts drifted where they always drifted.

Backward.

To the place she tried so hard not to revisit.

By the time she arrived home, exhaustion settled over her shoulders.

She unlocked the door and stepped inside.

The house was immaculate.

Everything in its place.

Everything under control.

Everything except her thoughts.

She dropped her purse onto the kitchen island and stopped.

An envelope rested beside the fruit bowl.

Her brow furrowed.

She hadn't left it there.

Carefully she approached.

Her name was written across the front in elegant gold lettering.

Bathsheba.

Not her legal name.

The other name.

The one she carried in silence.

The name connected to a story she had spent years trying to understand.

Trying to survive.

Slowly she opened the envelope.

Inside was a cream-colored card.

Simple.

Elegant.

Three words appeared in bold script.

BOARD THE BUS.

Below them:

Destination: The Kingdom.

Bathsheba blinked.

"What is this?"

She turned the card over.

Nothing.

No instructions.

No explanation.

No signature.

Only the invitation.

She laughed softly.

Then frowned.

Then read it again.

And again.

For reasons she couldn't explain, her heart began to race.

The invitation felt personal.

As though someone knew her.

Not the polished version.

The real version.

The woman beneath the accomplishments.

The woman beneath the success.

The woman still carrying shame.

She thought of the others who must have received this same card.

Women who had been discarded.

Women who had been overlooked.

Women who had spent years looking backward.

Women who had carried burdens too heavy for one person.

None of them had been forgotten.

Maybe she hadn't been either.

That night sleep came quickly.

The dream arrived almost immediately.

She stood in a palace courtyard.

Torches flickered against stone walls.

Footsteps echoed in the distance.

A woman stood alone beneath the stars.

Beautiful.

Broken.

Grieving.

Bathsheba recognized her instantly.

The biblical Bathsheba.

The woman history often reduced to a scandal.

A temptation.

A mistake.

But the dream revealed something deeper.

The loss.

The sorrow.

The consequences.

The years of carrying pain.

Then the scene shifted.

The woman grew older.

Wiser.

Stronger.

No longer defined by her worst moment.

No longer trapped by her past.

The dream changed again.

A crown appeared.

A kingdom.

A future.

Redemption.

A voice echoed through the night.

"You are more than your failure."

The words pierced her heart.

Again, the voice spoke.

"I redeemed what shame tried to destroy."

Bathsheba woke suddenly.

Tears covered her cheeks.

The room was dark.

The invitation sat on her nightstand.

Waiting.

For the next three days she carried the card everywhere.

Something about it refused to leave her thoughts.

Every meeting.

Every conversation.

Every quiet moment.

The invitation lingered.

By the fourth morning, she found herself standing at an unfamiliar bus station.

Women gathered nearby holding invitations identical to hers.

Some looked hopeful.

Others nervous.

Several appeared wounded.

Searching.

Broken.

Just like her.

Through the large windows of the bus, she could see women already seated inside.

One with warm brown eyes and a quiet stillness about her.

One gripping a leather planner as though releasing it might cost her something.

One clutching a worn cardboard box in her lap.

One with a heavy bag covered in small paper tags.

One with a large leather satchel resting at her feet, her shoulders finally beginning to drop.

Five women.

Five stories.

Five invitations answered.

And none of them looked like they had arrived without a wound.

Something about that steadied her.

Then she saw the bus.

Its polished exterior gleamed beneath the morning sun.

Above the windshield glowed a destination sign.

THE KINGDOM.

Her breath caught.

A strange sense of peace settled over her.

For the first time in years, she wasn't thinking about her past.

She was thinking about what might lie ahead.

The bus doors opened.

A warm voice called out.

"Welcome, daughters."

One by one the women began boarding.

Bathsheba remained still.

Fear tightened in her chest.

Not fear of the journey.

Fear of exposure.

What if everyone knew?

What if her secrets followed her here too?

Then she noticed something hanging from her shoulder.

A large velvet garment bag.

Heavy.

Much heavier than it should have been.

She unzipped it.

Inside were labels.

Hundreds of them.

Shame.

Failure.

Guilty.

Unworthy.

Damaged.

Disqualified.

Every accusation she had carried for years.

Every lie she secretly believed.

The weight nearly brought her to her knees.

The Driver appeared in the doorway.

His eyes rested on the garment bag.

Then on her.

No judgment.

No condemnation.

Only compassion.

Only understanding.

Only love.

"We've been expecting you, Bathsheba."

The words broke something inside her.

Not painfully.

Beautifully.

Because for years she had believed she needed to hide.

Yet somehow the Driver already knew everything.

And still welcomed her.

Still called her by name.

Bathsheba tightened her grip on the garment bag.

She wasn't ready to surrender it.

Not yet.

But for the first time, she *wanted* to.

Slowly she stepped forward.

One step.

Then another.

As she crossed the threshold of the bus, the burden seemed slightly lighter.

Not gone.

But lighter.

She moved down the aisle.

As she passed each woman, eyes lifted to meet hers.

No one spoke.

No one needed to.

Each woman carried something she wasn't ready to release.

Each woman had come anyway.

That was enough.

Bathsheba found an empty seat near the back and settled in.

She looked out the window one final time.

The station was nearly empty now.

The morning light had grown warmer.

The road ahead stretched farther than she could see.

The doors closed behind her.

The engine rumbled to life.

And deep within her heart, a new possibility began to emerge.

What if redemption was stronger than shame?

The road stretched ahead.

Six women now sat aboard a bus bound for the Kingdom.

Each carrying something she wasn't ready to release.

Each chosen before she fully understood what that meant.

Each seen by a Driver who had known her name long before she arrived.

And Bathsheba's journey toward forgiveness had finally begun.

CHAPTER SEVEN
The Invitation—Elizabeth

Elizabeth sat on the porch swing as the sun disappeared beyond the horizon.

The evening air carried the scent of freshly cut grass and blooming jasmine.

Somewhere down the street, children laughed as they chased one another across a front yard.

Elizabeth smiled.

The sound was beautiful.

And painful.

She wrapped her cardigan tighter around her shoulders and watched the neighborhood settle into evening.

Lights flickered on in nearby homes.

Families gathered around dinner tables.

Grandchildren visited grandparents.

Life moved forward.

As it always had.

As it always would.

At sixty-one years old, Elizabeth had learned to accept many things.

She had accepted growing older.

Accepted retirement.

Accepted living alone.

Accepted the quiet.

Most days she carried her disappointments gracefully.

Most days.

Tonight was not one of those days.

Her gaze drifted toward the old wooden box sitting beside the porch swing.

The box had traveled with her for nearly forty years.

Inside were reminders of prayers God had never answered.

At least that is what it had felt like.

Carefully she opened it.

A tiny pair of baby shoes rested on top.

Still white.

Still unworn.

Beneath them were journal entries.

Prayer cards.

Bible verses.

Letters written to a child she never had.

Her fingers trembled as she picked one up.

The date at the top was nearly thirty years old.

Dear Baby,

Today I prayed for you again…

Elizabeth closed her eyes.

The ache returned instantly.

For years she and her husband had prayed.

Believed.

Hoped.

Waited.

Month after month.

Year after year.

Appointment after appointment.

Disappointment after disappointment.

Eventually the doctors told them what neither wanted to hear.

Children would not come.

Not naturally.

Not miraculously.

Not at all.

At least that is what they believed.

Her husband had passed away five years earlier.

A good man.

A faithful man.

Together they had learned how to survive disappointment.

But some losses never completely healed.

They simply became part of who you were.

A tear slipped down her cheek.

Elizabeth wiped it away before it could fall onto the letter.

"Lord," she whispered softly.

The prayer felt familiar.

A conversation decades in the making.

"I know You're good."

The words came slowly.

"I know You're faithful."

She paused.

The next words hurt.

"But I still don't understand."

Silence answered.

Not an uncomfortable silence.

Just the quiet presence she had grown accustomed to over the years.

The kind of silence that asked her to trust even when she didn't understand.

The kind of silence that had never actually been empty.

Eventually she closed the box.

The sun had completely disappeared now.

Darkness settled over the neighborhood.

Elizabeth rose from the swing and headed inside.

As she entered the kitchen, something immediately caught her attention.

An envelope rested in the center of the table.

Her brow furrowed.

She was certain it hadn't been there earlier.

Slowly she approached.

Her name was written across the front in elegant gold lettering.

Elizabeth.

The sight made her pause.

A strange warmth filled her chest.

Because Elizabeth wasn't merely her name.

It was her story.

A woman who had waited.

A woman who had hoped.

A woman who had wondered if God remembered.

She had always loved the biblical Elizabeth.

Faithful through silence.

Hopeful through barrenness.

Chosen even in her waiting.

She had never imagined she might share more than a name with her.

Carefully she opened the envelope.

Inside was a cream-colored card.

Simple.

Beautiful.

Three words appeared in bold script.

BOARD THE BUS.

Below them:

Destination: The Kingdom.

Elizabeth blinked.

"What in the world?"

She turned the card over.

Nothing.

No instructions.

No address.

No explanation.

Only the invitation.

Yet something about it stirred her heart.

Not confusion.

Recognition.

As though she had been expecting it.

As though a part of her had been waiting for this invitation her entire life.

She thought of the women who must have received the same envelope.

Women who had been sent away.

Women who had tried to control what they feared losing.

Women who had turned back when they should have moved forward.

Women who had been overlooked.

Women who had carried everyone else's burdens.

Women who had spent years outrunning their past.

Each of them had been found.

Each of them had been called.

Perhaps waiting had never been a sign of being forgotten.

Perhaps it had been preparation.

That night she fell asleep with the card resting on her nightstand.

And she dreamed.

She stood in a temple illuminated by golden light.

An elderly woman knelt in prayer.

Her face reflected both hope and heartbreak.

Years seemed to pass in moments.

The woman continued praying.

Continued believing.

Continued waiting.

Elizabeth recognized her immediately.

The biblical Elizabeth.

Faithful.

Patient.

Forgotten by many.

Never forgotten by God.

The dream shifted.

The older woman touched her stomach.

A miracle had begun.

Life where there had been barrenness.

Promise where there had been disappointment.

Joy, where there had been waiting.

The scene changed again.

The woman held a child in her arms.

Tears streamed down her face.

Not because of the child.

Because God had remembered.

A voice echoed through the dream.

"I never forgot."

The words wrapped around Elizabeth's heart.

Again, the voice spoke.

"Waiting is not abandonment."

And then, quieter still.

"I was with you in every unanswered prayer."

Elizabeth woke with tears on her cheeks.

The room remained dark.

The invitation rested beside her bed.

Waiting.

Just as she had waited.

For the next three days, she carried the card everywhere.

The words lingered in her thoughts.

Board the Bus.

By the fourth morning, she found herself standing at an unfamiliar bus station.

Women gathered nearby holding invitations identical to hers.

Some appeared nervous.

Others excited.

A few looked wounded.

Searching.

Broken.

Yet every face carried the same unspoken question.

Why am I here?

Through the large windows of the bus, she could see women already seated inside.

One with warm brown eyes and a stillness that looked hard-won.

One with a leather planner resting in her lap, her grip slightly looser than it had been.

One clutching a worn cardboard box against her chest.

One with a heavy bag covered in paper tags, her shoulders beginning to soften.

One with a large leather satchel at her feet, her head bowed in quiet relief.

One with a velvet garment bag across her knees, her eyes fixed somewhere ahead.

Six women.

Six wounds.

Six invitations answered.

And not one of them had arrived empty-handed.

Then Elizabeth saw the bus.

Its polished exterior gleamed beneath the morning sun.

Above the windshield glowed a destination sign.

THE KINGDOM.

Her breath caught.

Peace settled over her heart.

Not excitement.

Not fear.

Peace.

The kind that comes after years of wrestling with unanswered questions.

The bus doors opened.

A warm voice called out.

"Welcome, daughters."

One by one the women began boarding.

Elizabeth remained still.

Not because she was afraid.

Because she noticed something at her feet.

The wooden box.

The same box she had carried for decades.

The box filled with unanswered prayers.

Unfulfilled dreams.

Questions.

Disappointments.

Carefully she picked it up.

The weight surprised her.

Not physically.

Emotionally.

She had carried it so long she no longer noticed how heavy it had become.

The Driver appeared in the doorway.

His eyes rested briefly on the box.

Then on her.

Compassion filled His face.

Deep.

Gentle.

Knowing.

"We've been expecting you, Elizabeth."

The words settled over her like sunlight.

Expected.

Not forgotten.

Not overlooked.

Expected.

Wanted.

Remembered.

Tears filled her eyes.

Because for the first time she wondered if God had remembered her all along.

Not in spite of the waiting.

Through it.

Elizabeth tightened her grip on the box.

She wasn't ready to let it go.

Not yet.

But she stepped forward.

One step.

Then another.

As she climbed aboard the bus, the burden felt slightly lighter.

Not gone.

But lighter.

She moved down the aisle slowly.

As she passed each woman, eyes lifted to meet hers.

No words were exchanged.

None were needed.

Each woman understood.

Each woman had come carrying something she was not ready to release.

Each woman had come anyway.

Elizabeth found a seat and settled in.

She set the wooden box gently on her lap and rested her hands on top of it.

For the first time in decades, the box did not feel like evidence of what God had withheld.

It felt like a record of every prayer He had heard.

The doors closed behind her.

The engine rumbled to life.

And deep within her heart, hope stirred once again.

Perhaps waiting had never meant God was absent.

Perhaps waiting had been part of the journey all along.

Seven women now sat aboard a bus bound for the Kingdom.

Each carrying something she wasn't ready to release.

Each chosen before she fully understood what that meant.

Each seen by a Driver who had known her name long before she arrived.

And Elizabeth's journey from disappointment to fulfillment had finally begun.

CHAPTER EIGHT

The Invitation—Woman at the Well

The Woman at the Well always chose the table in the corner.

Not because it had the best view.

It didn't.

From there, she could see the kitchen door, the cash register, the bar, and most importantly, the entrance.

She liked knowing who was coming before they saw her.

Old habit.

Survival habit.

At thirty-eight years old, she had learned that people rarely walked into your life quietly.

Some entered smiling and left you wounded.

Some made promises under soft lighting and broke them in daylight.

Some loved the idea of you until the real you became inconvenient.

So, she watched doors.

At the restaurant, everyone called her dependable.

Funny.

Sharp.

The kind of woman who could make customers laugh even when her own heart was tired.

She managed schedules, corrected orders, handled complaints, soothed angry guests, and kept the staff from falling apart on busy nights.

She made multitasking look like an Olympic sport.

But when her shift ended, the laughter ended too.

That night, the restaurant had been packed.

Couples at every table.

Hands touching across candlelight.

Anniversary desserts.

Engagement smiles.

Soft voices.

Inside jokes.

Love everywhere.

Or at least the appearance of it.

She had smiled through all of it.

"Congratulations."

"Enjoy your evening."

"Let me get that for you."

"You two are beautiful together."

By closing time, her cheeks hurt from pretending.

When the final customer left, she locked the front door and leaned against it.

The restaurant was quiet now.

Too quiet.

The air smelled of lemon cleaner, coffee, and the faint sweetness of leftover dessert.

Chairs sat upside down on tables.

The bar lights glowed dimly.

Somewhere in the kitchen, water dripped steadily into the sink.

Drip. Drip. Drip.

The sound irritated her.

Then saddened her.

She was thirsty.

Not for water.

For something she could not name.

Her phone buzzed in her apron pocket.

She pulled it out.

A message from a man she had promised herself she would stop answering.

You up?

Two words.

No care.

No commitment.

No love.

Just access.

Her thumb hovered over the screen.

She hated that part of herself.

The part that knew better but still wanted to feel wanted.

The part that confused attention with affection.

The part that would rather accept crumbs than sit alone with hunger.

She turned the phone face down on the bar.

"No," she whispered, though no one had asked the question aloud.

The word felt small.

But it was a beginning.

She finished closing, gathered her purse, and stepped into the night.

The city air was cool against her skin.

Streetlights reflected in puddles from an earlier rain.

Cars passed in streaks of white and red, everyone going somewhere, everyone belonging to someone.

At least that was how it seemed.

Her apartment was only ten minutes away, but the walk felt longer than usual.

She passed a church on the corner.

The sign out front read:

WHOEVER DRINKS THE WATER I GIVE WILL NEVER THIRST AGAIN.

She stopped.

The words reached for something inside her.

She looked away quickly.

Church signs were easy.

Life was harder.

By the time she reached her building, exhaustion had settled into her bones.

She climbed the stairs, unlocked her door, and stepped inside.

The apartment was neat.

Pretty, even.

Plants by the window.

Candles on the coffee table.

A soft blanket folded across the couch.

Everything arranged to look peaceful.

But peace did not live there.

Not yet.

She dropped her keys into the bowl near the door and froze.

An envelope rested on the small entry table.

She frowned.

It had not been there that morning.

No one had a key to her apartment.

No one should have been inside.

Slowly, she reached for it.

Her name was written across the front in elegant gold lettering.

Woman at the Well.

Her breath caught.

Not her legal name.

Not the name on her lease.

Not the name printed on her paychecks.

The name beneath all of it.

The woman who kept coming back thirsty.

The woman who had tried relationship after relationship, hoping one would finally satisfy what only God could fill.

With trembling fingers, she opened the envelope.

Inside was a cream-colored card.

Three words appeared in bold script.

BOARD THE BUS.

Beneath it:

Destination: The Kingdom.

She stared at the card.

Then laughed once, softly.

"What kind of mess is this?"

She turned it over.

Nothing.

No address.

No phone number.

No explanation.

Only the invitation.

She set it on the counter and walked away.

But the words followed her.

Board the Bus.

Destination: The Kingdom.

She thought about the women who must have received the same gold envelope.

Women who had been cast out into the wilderness.

Women who had tried to control everything and everyone around them.

Women who had refused to stop looking backward.

Women who had spent their whole lives being second.

Women who had poured themselves out for others until nothing remained.

Women who had spent years hiding behind accomplishment and shame.

Women who had waited so long they had nearly stopped believing.

And still, every one of them had been called.

Still, every one of them had been found.

Maybe she was not as far from that circle as she had believed.

That night, she dreamed.

She stood beneath a merciless noon sun, holding a water jar against her hip.

A dusty road stretched behind her.

A well stood ahead.

No crowd gathered there.

No women laughed nearby.

No one waited to walk with her.

She had chosen the hottest hour because loneliness was easier than judgment.

Then she saw Him.

A man seated by the well.

Waiting.

Not accidentally.

Intentionally.

He looked at her as though He already knew every chapter of her story.

Every man.

Every wound.

Every compromise.

Every lonely night.

Every thirst.

And still, He did not look away.

"Give Me a drink," He said.

The jar nearly slipped from her hands.

The dream shifted.

His voice became like water over stone.

"If you knew the gift of God…"

She woke before He finished.

Her room was dark.

Her heart was pounding.

The invitation sat on her nightstand.

She did not remember bringing it there.

For three days, she tried to ignore it.

She worked.

She laughed.

She dodged questions.

She deleted the man's message, then regretted it, then thanked God she had done it.

She walked past the church again.

The sign had changed.

Now it read:

COME AND SEE.

By the fourth morning, she stood at the bus station with the invitation folded in her hand.

She had no memory of deciding to come.

But there she was.

Other women gathered nearby.

Some looked polished.

Some looked weary.

Some clutched bags, boxes, planners, and suitcases.

Every woman seemed to carry something heavier than luggage.

Through the large windows of the bus, she could see women already seated inside.

One with warm brown eyes and a quiet, hard-won stillness.

One with a leather planner resting loosely in her lap.

One with a worn cardboard box held close to her chest.

One with a heavy bag of paper tags, her shoulders finally beginning to soften.

One with a leather satchel at her feet and a face that looked like it was learning to breathe again.

One with a velvet garment bag across her knees and eyes fixed on the road ahead.

One with an old wooden box resting gently in her lap, her hands folded on top as though in prayer.

Seven women.

Seven stories.

Seven invitations answered.

And not one of them had arrived without a wound.

Not one of them had arrived without a name.

Then she saw the bus.

It gleamed beneath the morning sun, its surface shining like it had been washed in light.

Above the windshield, the destination sign glowed softly.

THE KINGDOM.

Her throat tightened.

The bus doors opened.

A warm voice called from inside.

"Welcome, daughters."

One by one, the women began boarding.

The Woman at the Well stayed back.

She was used to being last.

Used to watching other women enter rooms confidently while she measured how much of herself to hide.

Then the Driver appeared in the doorway.

His eyes found hers.

Not accusing.

Not disappointed.

Not surprised.

Knowing.

He knew her.

All of her.

And somehow, that knowing did not feel like exposure.

It felt like invitation.

"We've been expecting you," He said.

Tears stung her eyes.

"Me?"

The Driver smiled.

"Yes. *You.*"

She looked down and realized she was holding something besides the invitation.

A water jar.

Clay.

Cracked.

Dry.

Empty.

Her fingers tightened around it.

The jar was familiar.

It was every relationship she had run to.

Every place she had tried to be filled.

Every thirst she had mistaken for love.

The Driver looked at the jar, then back at her.

He did not ask her to surrender it.

Not yet.

He only stepped aside and opened the way.

The Woman at the Well took one step forward.

Then another.

As she climbed onto the bus, the jar felt lighter in her hands.

She moved slowly down the aisle.

As she passed each woman, eyes lifted.

Some smiled softly.

Some simply nodded.

One reached out briefly and touched her arm.

I know.

Me too.

She found a seat near the window and settled in.

She held the empty jar in her lap and looked out at the road ahead.

The morning light was growing warmer.

Eight women.

Eight wounds.

Eight names written in gold.

Each carrying something she was not yet ready to release.

Each chosen before she understood what that meant.

Each seen by a Driver who had known her name long before she arrived.

The doors closed behind her.

The engine rumbled to life.

And for the first time in years, she did not think about who was coming through the door.

She thought about where she was going.

For the first time in years, she wondered if emptiness was not the end of her story.

Maybe it was the place where Living Water could finally begin.

The road stretched ahead.

And the Woman at the Well's journey toward wholeness had finally begun.

CHAPTER NINE

The Invitation—Mary Magdalene

Mary Magdalene unlocked the church doors before sunrise.

As usual.

The sanctuary was dark and silent except for the soft hum of the air conditioning.

Rows of empty pews stretched before her.

Most people would not arrive for another three hours.

But Mary was always early.

Always prepared.

Always serving.

She switched on the foyer lights and began her routine.

Coffee station.

Children's ministry supplies.

Welcome packets.

Bulletins.

Sound check.

Nursery inventory.

Volunteer schedules.

Every Sunday looked different.

Every Sunday felt exactly the same.

By eight o'clock the building would be filled with people.

Families.

Visitors.

Volunteers.

Pastors.

Worship teams.

Everyone would see the service.

Very few would see Mary.

She didn't resent it.

At least that was what she told herself.

For years she had been the dependable one.

The woman who never said no.

The woman who stayed late.

The woman who filled gaps.

The woman who made everything work behind the scenes.

People appreciated her.

They just rarely noticed her.

A familiar voice interrupted her thoughts.

"Morning, Mary."

She turned and smiled.

"Morning."

The associate pastor hurried past carrying notes for his sermon.

"Thank you for getting everything ready."

"Of course."

Then he was gone.

The interaction lasted less than ten seconds.

Yet it somehow summarized the last fifteen years of her life.

Necessary.

Helpful.

Forgettable.

By noon, the service was over.

The church buzzed with activity.

People laughed in the hallways.

Children ran through the lobby.

Families gathered for lunch.

Mary cleaned.

Straightened chairs.

Collected trash.

Restocked supplies.

As she carried a box toward the storage room, she overheard a conversation nearby.

The worship leader was thanking volunteers.

Names were mentioned.

Recognition was given.

Stories were shared.

Mary listened quietly.

Her name never came up.

The disappointment surprised her.

Not because she wanted applause.

Because she wanted to matter.

The realization followed her home.

By evening she sat alone on the porch of her small townhouse watching the sun disappear.

She felt guilty.

Faithful people shouldn't need recognition.

Faithful people should serve simply because they love God.

Yet deep inside, another truth existed.

She was tired of being invisible.

Tired of pouring herself out.

Tired of wondering if anyone noticed.

The thought made her uncomfortable.

So she prayed.

"Lord, forgive me."

The words barely escaped her lips.

"I know this isn't about me."

But another prayer followed.

One she hadn't planned to say.

"Do You see me?"

The question lingered in the evening air.

No answer came.

At least not immediately.

As darkness settled over the neighborhood, Mary rose and headed inside.

The house greeted her with familiar quiet.

She placed her keys on the kitchen counter and froze.

An envelope rested beside them.

Her heart skipped.

She knew it hadn't been there earlier.

Slowly she picked it up.

Her name appeared across the front in elegant gold lettering.

Mary Magdalene.

Not simply Mary.

Mary Magdalene.

The woman who had followed Jesus.

The woman who stayed.

The woman who witnessed.

The woman who loved deeply.

The woman who was the first to carry the news of resurrection.

A name that carried more than she had allowed herself to remember.

Carefully she opened the envelope.

Inside was a cream-colored card.

Simple.

Beautiful.

Three words appeared in bold script.

BOARD THE BUS.

Beneath them:

Destination: The Kingdom.

Mary stared.

"What bus?"

She turned the card over.

Nothing.

No explanation.

No directions.

No signature.

Only the invitation.

For reasons she couldn't explain, tears filled her eyes.

Because something about the invitation felt personal.

Intentional.

As though someone had written it specifically for her.

Not for the volunteer.

Not for the coordinator.

For her.

She thought of the women who must have received the same gold envelope.

Women who had been cast into the wilderness with nothing.

Women who had tried to control the very promises of God.

Women who had spent decades looking backward at what they had lost.

Women who had spent their whole lives being second in someone else's story.

Women who had poured themselves out until they had nothing left to give.

Women who had carried shame like a second skin.

Women who had waited so long they had nearly stopped believing.

Women who had confused thirst for love and kept returning to empty wells.

Every one of them had been found.

Every one of them had been called.

Perhaps she was no different.

That night she dreamed.

She stood outside ancient city walls.

The sky was dark.

A crowd gathered nearby.

A cross stood on a hill.

Most people were leaving.

Walking away.

Returning to their lives.

But a small group remained.

Women.

Faithful women.

Women who refused to abandon Jesus.

Among them stood Mary Magdalene.

Grieving.

Heartbroken.

Yet still present.

Still faithful.

The dream shifted.

Morning arrived.

The tomb appeared.

Stone rolled away.

Angels.

Light.

Wonder.

Then Mary Magdalene heard a voice.

One word.

Her name.

"Mary."

The sound carried such love that it broke her heart open.

The biblical Mary turned.

And immediately recognized Him.

The risen Christ.

The dream froze.

Then another voice echoed through the scene.

"You were never unseen."

The words wrapped around her soul.

Again, the voice spoke.

"Faithfulness is never forgotten."

And then, quieter still.

"I called your name first."

Mary woke with tears streaming down her face.

The invitation rested on her nightstand.

Waiting.

Just as she had waited.

For three days she couldn't stop thinking about it.

Every volunteer meeting.

Every worship service.

Every quiet evening.

The invitation remained in her thoughts.

Board the Bus.

Destination: The Kingdom.

By the fourth morning, she found herself standing at a bus station unlike any she had ever seen.

Women gathered nearby holding identical invitations.

Some appeared nervous.

Others hopeful.

Several looked wounded.

Searching.

Waiting.

Through the large windows of the bus, she could see women already seated inside.

One with warm brown eyes and a quiet, hard-won stillness.

One with a leather planner resting loosely in her lap.

One with a worn cardboard box held close to her chest.

One with a heavy bag of paper tags, her shoulders finally beginning to soften.

One with a leather satchel at her feet and a face that was learning to breathe again.

One with a velvet garment bag across her knees and eyes fixed on the road ahead.

One with an old wooden box resting gently in her lap, hands folded on top as though in prayer.

One with a cracked clay water jar held carefully in both hands, her gaze turned toward the window.

Eight women.

Eight stories.

Eight invitations answered.

And not one of them had arrived without a wound.

Not one of them had arrived without a name.

Then Mary saw the bus.

Its polished exterior gleamed beneath the morning sun.

Above the windshield glowed a destination sign.

THE KINGDOM.

A sense of peace settled over her.

Not excitement.

Not fear.

Belonging.

The bus doors opened.

A warm voice called out.

"Welcome, daughters."

One by one the women began boarding.

Mary remained where she stood.

Then she noticed something hanging from her shoulder.

A volunteer badge.

Old and worn.

Attached to it were dozens of smaller badges.

Teacher.

Helper.

Coordinator.

Volunteer.

Servant.

Worker.

Titles she had worn for years.

The badge grew heavier with every label.

As though her identity had become tied to what she did rather than who she was.

As though she had forgotten that Jesus had called her by name long before He gave her anything to do.

The Driver appeared in the doorway.

His eyes met hers.

Warm.

Kind.

Knowing.

Noticing.

The kind of gaze that saw beneath every title.

Every role.

Every responsibility.

"We've been expecting you, Mary."

The words struck her deeply.

Expected.

Known.

Seen.

Not because of what she had done.

Because of who she was.

Tears filled her eyes.

She looked down at the collection of badges.

The Driver glanced toward them.

Then back at her.

His smile remained gentle.

Not yet.

She wasn't ready to lay them down.

But she could take the next step.

Slowly Mary climbed aboard.

One step.

Then another.

As she crossed the threshold, the badges seemed slightly lighter.

Not gone.

But lighter.

She moved down the aisle slowly.

As she passed each woman, eyes lifted.

Some smiled softly.

Some simply nodded.

One reached out briefly and touched her arm.

I know.

Me too.

She found a seat and settled in.

The badges still hung from her shoulder.

But for the first time, she was not defined by them.

For the first time, she sat not as a volunteer, a coordinator, or a servant.

She sat as a daughter.

Chosen.

Expected.

Beloved.

The doors closed behind her.

The engine rumbled to life.

Nine women now sat aboard a bus bound for the Kingdom.

Each carrying something she was not yet ready to release.

Each chosen before she fully understood what that meant.

Each seen by a Driver who had known her name long before she arrived.

And deep within her heart, a new truth began to emerge.

Perhaps her value had never been found in service.

Perhaps it had always been found in being loved.

The road stretched ahead.

And Mary Magdalene's journey from unseen servant to beloved daughter had finally begun.

CHAPTER TEN
The Invitation—The Submissive Wife (Priscilla)

Priscilla sat alone at the kitchen table long after midnight.

The house was quiet.

Not peaceful.

Quiet.

The kind of silence that follows years of conversations left unfinished.

The kind of silence that settles over a home after too many words have gone unsaid.

A single lamp illuminated the room.

Bills lay scattered across the table.

A half-finished cup of tea sat untouched beside them.

Across the room, a clock ticked steadily.

Priscilla listened to it.

Tick. Tick. Tick.

Time moving forward.

Even when she felt stuck.

She rubbed her temples and closed her eyes.

Forty-four years old.

Business owner.

Mother.

Church leader.

Survivor.

Yet some days she still felt like the frightened young woman she had once been.

The woman who learned early that peace often came at the cost of her own voice.

For nearly twenty years she had been married to a man who made every decision.

Not with violence.

Not with shouting.

Something subtler.

Something harder to explain.

Control disguised as leadership.

Domination disguised as protection.

Silence disguised as submission.

Over time she stopped expressing opinions.

Stopped sharing dreams.

Stopped disagreeing.

Stopped asking for what she needed.

It seemed easier.

Safer.

Holier.

At least that's what she had believed.

People at church often praised her.

"You're such a godly wife."

"Such a submissive woman."

"Such a beautiful example."

The compliments always made her uncomfortable.

Because they didn't know the truth.

They didn't know how much of herself she had lost trying to become what everyone expected.

The marriage had ended three years earlier.

The divorce had been painful.

Necessary.

And confusing.

Even now she wrestled with guilt.

Had she failed?

Had she given up too soon?

Had she misunderstood God?

The questions lingered long after the papers were signed.

Priscilla reached for her Bible.

The worn leather cover felt familiar beneath her fingers.

She opened it to a passage she had read countless times.

"Wives, submit yourselves to your own husbands..."

Her eyes stopped there.

As they often did.

She knew the verse.

Had lived beneath its weight for decades.

Yet tonight her gaze drifted lower.

"...submit to one another out of reverence for Christ."

The words settled differently.

Mutual submission.

Mutual honor.

Mutual love.

A partnership.

Not oppression.

Not erasure.

The realization both comforted and unsettled her.

She closed the Bible gently.

The room felt heavy.

Not with condemnation.

With possibility.

As she stood to put away the dishes, something caught her attention.

An envelope rested on the kitchen counter.

Her brow furrowed.

She was certain it hadn't been there earlier.

Slowly she approached.

Her name appeared across the front in elegant gold lettering.

Priscilla.

The sight made her pause.

Not because of the handwriting.

Because of the name.

Priscilla.

A woman from Scripture.

Strong.

Wise.

A teacher.

A ministry partner.

A woman who worked alongside her husband rather than beneath him.

A woman whose voice mattered.

A woman who was never asked to disappear.

She had always admired the biblical Priscilla.

She had never imagined she might share more than a name with her.

Carefully she opened the envelope.

Inside was a cream-colored card.

Simple.

Elegant.

Three words appeared in bold script.

BOARD THE BUS.

Beneath them:

Destination: The Kingdom.

Priscilla blinked.

"What bus?"

She turned the card over.

Nothing.

No address.

No directions.

No explanation.

Only the invitation.

Yet something about it stirred her spirit.

Not fear.

Recognition.

As though she had been waiting for this invitation without realizing it.

She thought of the women who must have received the same gold envelope.

Women sent away with nothing.

Women who had tried to control what they feared losing.

Women who had turned back when they should have moved forward.

Women who had spent their whole lives being overlooked.

Women who had carried everyone else's weight until their own shoulders gave out.

Women who had hidden behind shame for years.

Women who had waited so long that hope had grown thin.

Women who had confused love with access and kept returning to empty places.

Women who had served faithfully and invisibly until they forgot their own names.

Every one of them had been called by name.

Every one of them had been expected.

Perhaps she was no different.

That night she dreamed.

She stood in an ancient home illuminated by oil lamps.

A woman taught Scripture to a small gathering.

Her voice was steady.

Confident.

Respected.

Men listened.

Women listened.

Children listened.

The woman wasn't apologizing for taking up space.

Wasn't shrinking herself.

Wasn't hiding her gifts.

Priscilla recognized her immediately.

The biblical Priscilla.

A partner in ministry.

A teacher.

A leader.

A daughter of God who knew her worth.

The dream shifted.

The room dissolved.

Now she stood in a vast field.

Chains lay scattered at her feet.

Invisible chains.

Fear.

People-pleasing.

Silence.

False guilt.

The chains began falling away one by one.

A voice echoed across the field.

"I never asked you to disappear."

Tears filled her eyes.

The voice spoke again.

"Submission was never meant to cost you your identity."

And then, quieter still.

"I made you be fully yourself."

The words pierced her heart.

Years of confusion.

Years of shame.

Years of misunderstanding.

All exposed in a single moment.

All held without condemnation.

Priscilla woke with tears on her cheeks.

The invitation rested beside her bed.

Waiting.

Just as she had waited.

For the next three days, she carried the card everywhere.

Something about it refused to leave her thoughts.

Every meeting.

Every client call.

Every quiet moment.

The invitation remained.

Board the Bus.

Destination: The Kingdom.

By the fourth morning, she found herself standing at an unfamiliar bus station.

Women gathered nearby holding identical invitations.

Some appeared nervous.

Others hopeful.

Several looked wounded.

Searching.

Waiting.

Through the large windows of the bus, she could see women already seated inside.

One with warm brown eyes and a quiet, hard-won stillness.

One with a leather planner resting loosely in her lap.

One with a worn cardboard box held close to her chest.

One with a heavy bag of paper tags, her shoulders finally beginning to soften.

One with a leather satchel at her feet and a face learning to breathe again.

One with a velvet garment bag across her knees and eyes fixed on the road ahead.

One with an old wooden box resting gently in her lap, hands folded on top as though in prayer.

One with a cracked clay water jar held carefully in both hands, her gaze turned toward the window.

One with a cluster of worn volunteer badges hanging from her shoulder, her face finally beginning to soften into something that looked like rest.

Nine women.

Nine stories.

Nine invitations answered.

And not one of them had arrived without a wound.

Not one of them had arrived without a name.

Then she saw the bus.

Its polished exterior gleamed beneath the morning sun.

Above the windshield glowed a destination sign.

THE KINGDOM.

Her breath caught.

Peace settled over her.

Not because she understood where she was going.

Because for the first time in years she wasn't trying to earn her place.

The bus doors opened.

A warm voice called out.

"Welcome, daughters."

One by one the women began boarding.

Priscilla remained where she stood.

Then she noticed something wrapped around her shoulders.

A heavy shawl.

Gray.

Worn.

Far heavier than fabric should have been.

When she looked closely, words appeared embroidered throughout the cloth.

Stay Quiet.

Don't Make Waves.

Be Smaller.

Keep Everyone Happy.

Your Needs Don't Matter.

The weight nearly brought her to tears.

She had carried these messages for so long they felt normal.

She had mistaken their heaviness for holiness.

The Driver appeared in the doorway.

His eyes rested briefly on the shawl.

Then on her.

Compassion filled His face.

Not judgment.

Not disappointment.

Understanding.

As though He knew every compromise she had made.

Every tear she had hidden.

Every piece of herself she had sacrificed.

Every prayer she had whispered in the dark wondering if God had confused her silence for contentment.

"We've been expecting you, Priscilla."

The words settled deep within her heart.

Expected.

Not tolerated.

Not merely accepted.

Expected.

Wanted.

Known.

Priscilla tightened her grip on the shawl.

She wasn't ready to remove it.

Not yet.

But she stepped forward.

One step.

Then another.

As she climbed aboard the bus, the shawl felt slightly lighter.

Not gone.

But lighter.

She moved slowly down the aisle.

As she passed each woman, eyes lifted to meet hers.

Some smiled softly.

Some simply nodded.

One reached out and briefly touched her hand.

I know.

Me too.

She found a seat and settled in.

The shawl still rested across her shoulders.

But for the first time, she was not defined by its weight.

For the first time, she sat not as a wife, a survivor, or a woman who had learned to make herself small.

She sat as a daughter.

Chosen.

Expected.

Fully herself.

The doors closed behind her.

The engine rumbled to life.

Ten women now sat aboard a bus bound for the Kingdom.

Each carrying something she was not yet ready to release.

Each one chosen before they fully understood the meaning.

Each seen by a Driver who had known her name long before she arrived.

And somewhere deep within her soul, a new truth began to emerge.

Perhaps God never wanted her to lose herself in order to serve Him.

Perhaps He had been calling her to become fully herself all along.

The road stretched ahead.

And Priscilla's journey from silence to freedom had finally begun.

CHAPTER ELEVEN

The Invitation—Jezebel

Jezebel liked being the last person in the building.

It reminded her of who was in charge.

The corner office on the twenty-third floor overlooked the city. Beneath the glass walls, thousands of lights stretched across the skyline like a sea of stars. Most people found the view inspiring.

Jezebel found it reassuring.

From here, everything looked small.

Manageable.

Controllable.

The way she preferred it.

She stood beside the window, arms crossed, watching the city move below her.

Her company had just finalized the largest contract in its history.

The board was thrilled.

Investors were celebrating.

Her employees practically worshiped her.

Tomorrow her photograph would appear on the cover of a business magazine.

Another award.

Another accomplishment.

Another victory.

Yet the office felt strangely empty.

Jezebel ignored the feeling.

She had learned long ago that emotions were liabilities.

Needs were weaknesses.

Vulnerability was dangerous.

Power kept people safe.

Power kept people respected.

Power kept people from leaving.

At least that was what she told herself.

Her phone buzzed.

The screen illuminated with her sister's name.

She stared at it.

The call went to voicemail.

A moment later, a text appeared.

Mom asked about you today.

Jezebel rolled her eyes.

Another guilt trip.

Another attempt to pull her back into family drama.

She deleted the message.

Then immediately regretted it.

Not because she wanted to respond.

Because the regret reminded her that somewhere beneath the armor, she still cared.

And caring always complicated things.

The office suddenly felt too quiet.

She returned to her desk and opened a file.

Then another.

Work solved everything.

Work filled silence.

Work prevented reflection.

Reflection was dangerous.

Reflection led to memories.

Memories led to pain.

And pain led to weakness.

The chain was simple.

So, she stayed busy.

Hours later, long after everyone else had gone home, she finally shut down her computer.

As she gathered her belongings, her gaze drifted toward a framed photograph sitting at the back of her bookshelf.

Most people never noticed it.

She rarely looked at it herself.

A younger Jezebel smiled from the picture.

Before the promotions.

Before the awards.

Before the walls.

Before betrayal taught her that trust was expensive.

She quickly looked away.

The memory hurt more than she expected.

The drive home was silent.

No music.

No radio.

Only headlights cutting through the darkness.

Her penthouse apartment greeted her with luxury.

Marble floors.

Floor-to-ceiling windows.

Designer furniture.

Everything carefully chosen.

Everything beautiful.

Everything empty.

Jezebel tossed her keys onto the kitchen island.

The sound echoed through the spacious room.

For a moment she wondered what all the success was actually for.

The thought irritated her.

Success didn't need a purpose.

Success was the purpose.

Yet the question lingered.

Before she could think further, something caught her attention.

An envelope rested in the center of the kitchen counter.

Her brow furrowed.

She lived alone.

No one had access to the apartment.

Slowly she approached.

Her name was written across the front in elegant gold lettering.

Jezebel.

The sight annoyed her immediately.

Not because of the handwriting.

Because of the name.

A name people used carelessly.

A name people attached to assumptions.

A name associated with manipulation, control, and destruction.

Yet no one ever asked why.

No one ever asked what created a woman like Jezebel.

They only judged the outcome.

With a sigh, she opened the envelope.

Inside was a cream-colored card.

Simple.

Elegant.

Three words appeared in bold script.

BOARD THE BUS.

Below them:

Destination: The Kingdom.

Jezebel laughed.

Actually laughed.

"What kind of nonsense is this?"

She turned the card over.

Nothing.

No explanation.

No directions.

No signature.

Only the invitation.

She tossed it onto the counter and walked away.

Five minutes later, she returned and picked it up again.

Something about it bothered her.

Not because it was strange.

Because it felt personal.

As though someone knew her.

Not the public version.

The private version.

The woman beneath the accomplishments.

The woman beneath the control.

The woman she spent years hiding.

She thought of all the women who must have received the same gold envelope.

Women sent away with nothing and no one.

Women who had tried to manage what they feared losing.

Women who had looked backward when they should have moved forward.

Women who had spent their lives being invisible, overlooked, exhausted.

Women who had carried shame like a second skin.

Women who had waited until hope grew thin.

Women who had confused access for love.

Women who had served faithfully while slowly disappearing.

Women who had made themselves smaller and smaller until they forgot their own shape.

Every one of them had been expected.

Every one of them had been known.

She wondered if she was any different.

She set the card down carefully.

For once, she didn't have an answer.

That night she dreamed.

She stood inside a palace.

Golden walls surrounded her.

Servants moved through the halls.

Power radiated from every corner.

A queen sat upon a throne.

Confident.

Commanding.

Untouchable.

Jezebel recognized her immediately.

The biblical Jezebel.

Strong.

Influential.

Feared.

The scene shifted.

The queen stood alone.

The throne room emptied.

The power remained.

But the relationships disappeared.

The influence remained.

But intimacy vanished.

The crown suddenly looked heavy.

Lonely.

The dream shifted again.

The queen reached toward something.

Love.

Trust.

Connection.

Yet every time she reached, the armor surrounding her prevented her from touching it.

A voice echoed through the palace.

"What you call strength has become a prison."

The words struck like thunder.

Again, the voice spoke.

"You cannot receive love while wearing armor."

And then, quieter still.

"I did not make you to be feared. I made you to be loved."

The palace began to crumble.

The throne disappeared.

The crown fell.

Only the woman remained.

Alone.

Afraid.

Human.

Jezebel woke abruptly.

Her heart pounded.

The room was dark.

The invitation rested on her nightstand.

Waiting.

For three days she couldn't stop thinking about the dream.

Or the invitation.

Every board meeting.

Every interview.

Every conversation.

The words followed her.

Board the Bus.

Destination: The Kingdom.

By the fourth morning she found herself standing at a bus station.

The decision irritated her.

She didn't even know why she came.

Other women gathered nearby holding invitations identical to hers.

Some looked nervous.

Others hopeful.

Several appeared wounded.

Jezebel immediately noticed weaknesses.

Insecurities.

Fears.

The things she spent years training herself to conceal.

Through the large windows of the bus, she could see women already seated inside.

One with warm brown eyes and a quiet, hard-won stillness.

One with a leather planner resting loosely in her lap.

One with a worn cardboard box held close to her chest.

One with a heavy bag of paper tags, her shoulders finally beginning to soften.

One with a leather satchel at her feet and a face learning to breathe again.

One with a velvet garment bag across her knees and eyes fixed on the road ahead.

One with an old wooden box resting gently in her lap, hands folded on top as though in prayer.

One with a cracked clay water jar held carefully in both hands, her gaze turned toward the window.

One with a cluster of worn volunteer badges hanging from her shoulder, her face finally beginning to soften into something that looked like rest.

One with a heavy embroidered shawl still wrapped around her shoulders, sitting a little straighter than she had in years.

Ten women.

Ten stories.

Ten invitations answered.

Jezebel studied them through the glass.

She expected to feel superior.

She did not.

She expected to feel nothing.

She felt something she could not name.

Then she saw the bus.

Its polished exterior gleamed beneath the morning sun.

Above the windshield glowed a destination sign.

THE KINGDOM.

The sight stirred something she couldn't identify.

Not excitement.

Not fear.

Curiosity.

The bus doors opened.

A warm voice called out.

"Welcome, daughters."

One by one, the women began boarding.

Jezebel remained where she stood.

Then she noticed something draped across her shoulders.

Armor.

Black.

Beautiful.

Heavy.

Far heavier than she realized.

The metal shimmered with engraved words.

Control.

Power.

Self-Reliance.

Protection.

Independence.

The armor had protected her for years.

It had also isolated her.

The Driver appeared in the doorway.

His eyes met hers.

Steady.

Patient.

Knowing.

As though He could see straight through every layer of steel. The Driver looked at her. Not at the armor, not at the reputation, not at the name they had made a weapon.

He looked at the woman underneath.

Not with judgment.

Not with condemnation.

With patience that had been waiting longer than she knew.

"I know what they call you," He said quietly. "That is not what I call you."

"I've been expecting you."

The words unsettled her.

Expected.

Known.

Seen.

Not feared.

Not used.

Not judged.

The Driver glanced briefly toward the armor.

Then back at her.

No condemnation.

No fear.

No intimidation.

Only truth.

Jezebel tightened her grip on the armor.

She wasn't ready to remove it.

Not yet.

Perhaps not ever.

But something compelled her forward.

One step.

Then another.

As she climbed aboard the bus, the armor felt slightly heavier.

Not lighter.

Heavier.

As though the journey itself would force her to acknowledge its weight.

She moved down the aisle.

As she passed each woman, a few eyes lifted to meet hers.

No fear.

No awe.

Recognition.

As though they already understood something she was only beginning to suspect.

That she was not so different from any of them.

She found a seat and settled in.

The armor pressed against her shoulders.

But for the first time, she sat not as the most powerful woman in the room.

She sat simply as a woman.

Invited.

Expected.

Known.

The doors closed behind her.

The engine rumbled to life.

Eleven women now sat aboard a bus bound for the Kingdom.

Each carrying something she was not yet ready to release.

Each chosen before she fully understood what that meant.

Each seen by a Driver who had known her name long before she arrived.

And somewhere deep inside, a battle began.

Not between good and evil.

But between control and surrender.

Between pride and humility.

Between self-protection and love.

The road stretched ahead.

And though she did not yet realize it, Jezebel's greatest enemy would not be the other passengers.

It would be the fortress she had built around her own heart.

CHAPTER TWELVE
The Invitation—Rachel

Rachel had always been the one people noticed first.

It was not something she asked for.

It was simply the way things were.

She walked into a room and heads turned. She posted a photo and the comments filled before she could put her phone down. She had the kind of life that looked effortless from the outside, and she had worked very hard to make sure it stayed that way.

She was loved.

She was chosen.

She was beautiful.

And still something was missing.

She could not name it at first.

It hid behind her busy schedule and her beautiful home and the way her husband still looked at her across a crowded room like she was the only person in it.

It hid behind her children's laughter and her carefully curated life and the quiet satisfaction of being the woman other women wanted to be.

But it was there.

A hollow place.

A low hum of hunger no amount of abundance could silence.

She had a sister named Leah.

They did not talk much about the distance between them.

It had grown so gradually that neither sister could point to the exact moment it began. It was easier to post a kind comment on each other's photos than to sit in the same room and say the things that needed to be said.

Rachel remembered the day she posted their family anniversary photo.

Her husband's arm around her.

The children laughing in the background.

The golden light catching everything just right.

The caption had come easily.

Five years of chosen. Five years of loved. Five years of grateful. #Blessed #StillMyPerson #FamilyFirst #GratefulHeart

The comments arrived quickly.

Hundreds of them.

Hearts.

Praise.

Relationship goals.

You two are everything.

She smiled reading them.

Each one.

Then she saw one small, quiet "like" from an account she almost scrolled past.

@LeahUnwavering.

No words.

Just a "like."

Rachel stared at it for a long moment.

Then she kept scrolling.

What Rachel did not know—what she could not have known—was what Leah had done before pressing that button.

Leah had looked at the photo for a long time.

She had seen the golden light and the laughing children and her sister's easy smile. She had felt the familiar ache move through her chest like weather.

And then, quietly, faithfully, without a single word, she had pressed "like."

Not because it was easy.

Because love sometimes looks like pressing "like" on a photo that costs you something.

Rachel did not know that.

She had kept scrolling.

But the hollow place would not be quiet.

Late at night, after the house had settled and the children were asleep and her husband's breathing had gone slow and even beside her, Rachel lay awake and scrolled.

She told herself she was just catching up.

Just staying connected.

Just seeing what people were doing.

But she knew what she was really doing.

Measuring.

A woman from her college years posted about a book deal.

A ministry leader announced a new campus.

A former colleague celebrated a promotion.

A family she had never met gathered around a table that looked like every holiday Rachel had ever wanted to host.

The comments always said the same things.

Goals.

Blessed.

Inspired.

Can't wait to get there.

Rachel scrolled past them with the particular efficiency of someone who had done this enough times to know exactly how it would feel and did it anyway.

She told herself she was happy for them.

She was.

She told herself the hollow place was not getting louder.

It was.

The invitation arrived on a Tuesday.

Rachel almost missed it.

It was tucked between a dry cleaning receipt and a stack of unopened mail she had been meaning to get to for weeks.

A small cream-colored envelope with her name written across the front in handwriting that felt somehow familiar, like a voice she had heard before but could not quite place.

She opened it slowly.

Inside was a single card.

Simple.

Cream-colored.

Beautiful.

Three words appeared in bold script.

BOARD THE BUS.

Below it:

Destination: The Kingdom.

Rachel stared at it.

She turned it over.

Nothing.

No address.

No sender.

No explanation.

Just the invitation.

She almost laughed.

"Well, that's certainly different."

She set it on the counter and returned to her evening routine.

But throughout the night, she found herself glancing at it.

Again.

And again.

Something about the card unsettled her.

Not in a frightening way.

In a familiar way.

As if someone who knew her completely had written it.

As if the handwriting belonged to someone who had been watching for a very long time and had finally decided to speak.

When she fell asleep that night, she dreamed.

She stood beside a well in a vast, dry land.

The sky above was enormous. The kind of sky that makes you feel small in a way that is not frightening but clarifying.

Around the well, other women gathered with their jars.

They talked.

They laughed.

They moved with the ease of people who knew their place in the world.

Rachel watched from a short distance.

In the dream she was beautiful.

Of course she was.

Even here, in this ancient place, she was the one people noticed first.

A man watched her from across the field with the particular attention of someone who had just seen something he did not expect and was not yet sure what to do about it.

She recognized the story.

Jacob.

The well.

The kiss.

The tears.

The promise.

I will work seven years for you.

The dream moved forward.

Years passed in the way dreams compress time. Not scene by scene, but in feeling.

In weight.

The years of waiting.

The years of watching her sister bear son after son while she remained empty.

The years of praying for the one thing she could not seem to have while the thing she already possessed—the love, the choosing, the man whose heart had always been hers—went unnoticed beneath the hunger.

Then the dream shifted.

She stood in a tent.

Alone.

Outside, she could hear Leah's children playing.

She could hear the ordinary sounds of a household that was full. Full of life, full of noise, full of the particular abundance that comes from being fruitful.

Inside the tent, Rachel sat with her hands in her lap.

Empty hands.

She looked down at them for a long time.

Then a voice filled the dream.

Not loud.

Not dramatic.

No thunder.

No wind.

Just present.

Close.

The way a voice sounds when it is speaking directly to you and no one else.

"What is it you are really hungry for?"

The question moved through her like light through water.

She opened her mouth to answer.

She did not have an answer.

The voice continued.

"You have been given much. You have been loved. You have been chosen. And still, you reach for what your sister carries, while your sister reaches for what you carry. Neither of you has stopped long enough to receive what I have placed in your own hands."

Rachel looked down again.

Her hands were no longer empty.

She was holding something.

She could feel its weight, warm and certain, but she could not quite see what it was, as though the dream was showing her the shape of the gift before it was ready to show her the gift itself.

The voice spoke once more.

"Come as you are. I have been waiting for you."

The dream ended.

Rachel woke up in the early hours of morning.

The room was dark.

Her husband slept beside her.

The house was quiet in the way houses are quiet when everything inside them is at rest.

She lay still for a long time.

The invitation sat on the nightstand.

She did not remember carrying it there.

She stared at the ceiling and thought about the dream.

The well.

The empty hands that were not empty.

The voice asking the question she had been running from for longer than she wanted to admit.

What is it you are really hungry for?

Then she thought about Leah.

About the quiet "like" from @LeahUnwavering.

About what it must have cost her sister to press that button.

What it must have felt like to look at that photo—the golden light, the laughing children, the man whose heart had always belonged to Rachel—and choose love anyway.

Choose presence.

Choose the small, faithful, uncelebrated act of pressing "like" and putting the phone face down.

Rachel had kept scrolling.

She had not deserved that "like."

She had barely even noticed it.

Something moved through her chest.

Not the hollow hunger.

Something different.

Something that felt, strangely, like the beginning of an answer.

By morning, she had made a decision.

Or perhaps the decision had been made somewhere inside her while she slept.

She told herself she was not going.

She had things to do.

She had a life that worked.

A reputation to maintain.

A schedule to keep.

People who depended on her to be exactly who she had always been.

But the hollow place would not be quiet.

And the handwriting on the envelope felt like something she had been waiting for without knowing she was waiting.

She packed a bag without fully deciding to.

She chose carefully the way she always did.

The right shoes.

The right coat.

The right bag that said I am put together even when she was not.

She stood in front of the mirror for a long moment and looked at the woman looking back.

Beautiful.

Chosen.

Loved.

Hollow.

"Come as you are," the voice had said.

Rachel looked at her reflection for one more moment.

Then she picked up the bag and walked out the door.

Three days after the invitation arrived, Rachel stood at a bus station unlike any she had ever seen.

Women gathered nearby, each holding an identical cream-colored invitation.

Some smiled nervously.

Others looked excited.

A few appeared afraid.

Rachel straightened instinctively. The reflex of a woman who had spent her life being looked at and had learned to manage what people saw.

Then she stopped.

Come as you are.

She let her shoulders drop.

She noticed the bus.

It was not what she expected.

She had imagined something grander. Something that matched the weight of the invitation.

Instead, it was quiet.

Steady.

Waiting in the early morning light without urgency, as though it had all the time in the world.

The destination sign above the windshield glowed softly.

THE KINGDOM.

Something shifted in her chest.

The bus doors opened.

A warm voice called from within.

"Welcome, daughters."

The women began boarding.

One by one.

Rachel remained where she was.

Not because she had decided against it.

Because something in her needed to stand there for one moment—to feel the full weight of what it meant to arrive somewhere as herself and not as the *performance* of herself.

The Driver appeared in the doorway.

He looked at her without surprise.

Without the look she was used to. The look that said there she is, the beautiful one, the chosen one, the one everyone notices first.

He did not look at her the way people looked at her.

He looked at her the way one looks at someone they have been waiting for.

With recognition.

With certainty.

With something that had nothing to do with how she appeared and everything to do with who she was.

"Rachel," He said.

Simply.

Completely.

Like her name was not a performance but a fact.

"I'm expected?" she asked.

The Driver smiled.

"You have always been expected."

Tears filled her eyes.

She thought of the hollow space.

The late-night scrolling.

The hundreds of comments.

The one quiet like she had scrolled past.

She thought of the dream. The empty hands that were not empty, the voice asking the question she had not yet answered.

She thought of Leah.

And she stepped onto the bus.

She moved down the aisle slowly, taking in the faces. Women she did not know, women carrying things she could not yet name.

Then she stopped.

Leah was there.

Her sister.

Sitting quietly near the window.

Not performing.

Not pretending.

Just present.

The way Leah had always been present, faithful and quiet and far too easy to overlook.

Rachel stood in the aisle for a long moment.

She thought about the anniversary post.

The golden light.

The hundreds of comments.

The one small "like" from @LeahUnwavering.

No words.

Just a "like."

Love sometimes looks like pressing "like" on a photo that costs you something.

Rachel felt the hollow place ache with something new.

Not hunger this time.

Recognition.

She walked to where Leah was sitting.

Leah looked up.

For a moment, Rachel saw something in her sister's eyes that made her chest tighten.

Not anger.

Not accusation.

Something worse.

Hope.

Careful hope.

The kind that had learned not to expect too much.

Rachel opened her mouth.

Nothing came.

There were words she needed to say.

Words she should have said years ago.

I didn't know.

I'm sorry.

I thought because you never complained, because you smiled, because you kept showing up, that you were okay.

But the words were too large for the aisle.

Too tender for the moment.

So, Rachel did the only thing she could do.

She sat down beside her sister.

Not across from her.

Not near her.

Beside her.

Leah did not move away.

Rachel noticed.

And because she noticed, something inside her began to break.

Not painfully.

Truthfully.

She looked at Leah.

Leah looked back.

For the first time in longer than either of them could remember, they were simply two sisters.

Not the beautiful one and the overlooked one.

Not the chosen one and the one who waited.

Not rivals.

Not reflections of each other's wounds.

Just sisters.

Sitting together.

On their way to something neither of them fully understood yet.

The bus began to move.

CHAPTER THIRTEEN

Baggage

Suitcases, Labels, Satchels, and Boxes—Hagar, Leah, Abigail, and Elizabeth

The bus rolled steadily along the Highway of Grace.

Morning light spilled through the windows, painting ribbons of gold across the aisle. Beyond the glass, the landscape had shifted entirely from what they had left behind. The cities and neighborhoods, the familiar streets, the crowded intersections—the places where each woman had built her life and her story—were gone.

Now rolling meadows stretched toward distant mountains. Crystal rivers glimmered beneath skies impossibly blue. Wildflowers bent gently in a breeze that seemed to come from somewhere beyond ordinary weather.

The scenery was beautiful.

Yet inside the bus, something felt different.

Heavier.

The Driver seemed quieter than usual. More watchful. As though He knew something the women did not. Something waiting just ahead on the road, patient and certain, that would require more from them than the boarding had.

Every woman had carried something onto the bus.

That much had been clear from the beginning. No one had boarded empty-handed. No one had arrived without the weight of her particular history pressing against her shoulders, tucked under her arm, gripped in both hands like something she was not yet ready to release.

Hagar sat near the middle of the bus, her old brown suitcase resting beside her seat. She had carried it since before she could remember.

She stared out the window at the passing countryside, but her attention kept returning to the suitcase the way one's tongue returns to a sore tooth. Involuntarily, helplessly, aware that pressing it would hurt and pressing it anyway.

She had never opened it. Not fully.

Something about it frightened her. As though she already knew what waited inside and was not yet certain she was strong enough to look.

Across the aisle, Leah sat quietly with a leather bag in her lap. It was covered in labels. Small, worn tags that fluttered in the still air of the cabin as though they had their own restless energy. The labels had been there so long that Leah had stopped reading them consciously. She simply carried them the way you carry a name you were given before you were old enough to choose your own.

The other women carried their burdens in their own ways.

Rebekah clutched her planner—leather-bound, color-coded, full of contingency plans for contingencies she had not yet imagined. Elizabeth held a wooden box in both hands, her knuckles pale against the grain. Priscilla wore a heavy shawl across her shoulders that seemed to weigh more than fabric should. Rachel held her mirror-filled handbag close against her side, one hand resting on the clasp as though something inside might escape if she relaxed her grip. Jezebel sat in her black armor—gleaming, impenetrable, sealed tight against everything that might get through. Bathsheba held a velvet garment bag draped across her knees. The Woman at the Well cradled her cracked clay jar. Mary Magdalene's worn volunteer badges hung from her shoulder in a cluster. Lot's Wife gripped a worn cardboard box with the careful attention of someone protecting something fragile. Abigail kept her leather satchel close, one hand resting on it the way she rested her hand on everything—steadily, practically, ready to manage whatever came next.

Twelve women.

Twelve burdens.

One bus.

> *"Before I formed you in the womb, I knew you; before you were born, I sanctified you." — Jeremiah 1:5 (NKJV)*

The bus slowed.

Conversations quieted. The subtle vibration of the engine softened. The Driver guided the bus to a gentle stop beside a vast field of wildflowers. Thousands of them stretched in every direction, their colors so vivid they seemed lit from within.

The Driver stood.

A warm smile rested on His face. Not the smile of someone about to deliver good news. The smile of someone who knows exactly what is needed, even when what is needed is difficult.

"Ladies."

Every head turned.

"It is time."

The women exchanged uncertain glances. Time for what? The wildflowers swayed outside. The sky was impossibly clear. Everything looked peaceful. Everything felt like the pause before something shifts.

The Driver pointed—not dramatically, not with urgency, simply, clearly—toward the luggage resting beside each woman.

"Your baggage."

A nervous laugh escaped Rachel.

"My baggage?"

"Yes."

Silence settled over the bus.

Then He continued, His voice unhurried and certain.

"You cannot enter the Kingdom carrying what was never meant to define you."

The words landed heavily. They had the particular weight of things that are true. The kind of true that does not argue with you, that simply stands in the room until you stop pretending it isn't there.

No one moved.

No one spoke.

The Driver waited.

He was very good at waiting.

Finally, Abigail broke the silence.

"What do You want us to do?"

The Driver smiled.

"Open them."

A collective groan filled the bus.

"No."

Rachel hugged her handbag tighter against her side.

"I don't think that's necessary."

Several women nodded with the particular enthusiasm of people who very much agreed and very much hoped the conversation would end there.

The Driver chuckled softly.

"It is."

The laughter faded.

One by one the women looked down at the burdens they carried. The bags and boxes and jars and armor and labels that had traveled with them from the lives they had left behind. The things they had packed without thinking because they had carried them so long, they no longer remembered a time before them.

Then Hagar noticed something.

The suitcase beside her had begun trembling.

Not violently. Not dramatically. Subtly—a low, steady vibration, as though something inside had finally run out of patience. As though the contents had been waiting for this moment longer than she had.

Her stomach tightened.

No.

She placed a hand on the lid. The trembling continued. She pressed down harder. The trembling did not stop.

Not today.

But even as she thought it, she understood that today was exactly the point.

Across the aisle, Leah stared at her own bag.

The labels on its surface had begun to flutter—not from any wind inside the bus, but from something else. Something that felt like the moment before a door opens. The tags rattled softly against one another:

Not Pretty Enough. Second Choice. Invisible. Unwanted. The One He Settled For.

Leah had read them so many times they had stopped feeling like accusations. They had simply become descriptions. The way *tall* describes a person or *quiet* describes a room. She had worn them for so long she had forgotten they were labels and not facts.

Then a latch clicked.

Leah gasped.

The bag opened.

Hundreds of labels spilled into the aisle, tumbling over one another, spreading across the floor of the bus in a cascade of small, worn tags. Every painful name she had ever believed about herself. Every word that had been spoken over her, withheld from her, or written across her life by someone else's choices.

The women watched in silence.

Leah's eyes filled with tears.

"I didn't realize there were this many," she said quietly.

Abigail moved to sit beside her. She looked down at the labels scattered across the floor and then back at Leah with an expression that was not pity. It was recognition.

"There aren't that many," Abigail said gently.

"Those are the same lies repeated over and over."

Leah looked up.

The words settled into the cabin like something long overdue. Leah looked at the labels again. Really looked at them, perhaps for the first time. Saw how many of them said the same thing in different arrangements. Saw how a handful of lies, repeated long enough, could fill an entire bag.

For the first time, she was not carrying them alone.

> *"The Lord has surely looked on my affliction. Now therefore, my husband will love me." — Genesis 29:32 (NKJV)*

Leah had named her sons after her longing.

She had written her wounds into the names of her children because there was nowhere else to put them. She had carried the labels so long she had forgotten who gave them to her. She had forgotten that they had been placed on her by circumstances and silences and a man whose heart lived somewhere else, not handed to her by the God who had opened her womb when everything else was closed.

They were never hers to keep.

She was beginning, slowly, to understand that.

Then another sound echoed through the bus.

Click.

Every head turned.

Hagar froze.

The latch on her suitcase had opened.

Her heart pounded. *No. Not yet. I'm not ready.*

But readiness, she was learning, was not always the prerequisite. Sometimes the door opened before you felt prepared to walk through it. Sometimes the truth emerged on its own schedule.

The lid lifted slowly.

The first item floated upward.

A photograph.

Hagar's breath caught in her throat. She and Marcus on their wedding day. She looked younger in it. Hopeful, certain, leaning into him with the particular confidence of someone who has not yet learned that love does not always stay.

Another photograph followed.

Her son. Age ten. Holding a baseball trophy. His gap-toothed grin aimed directly at the camera.

Then another. Her daughter. Missing front teeth. Laughing at something just outside the frame.

More items emerged.

Birthday cards. Mother's Day letters. Family photographs. Voicemails. Text messages. Memories. Years of memories rising from the suitcase like something that had been held underwater and finally released.

The bus grew very quiet.

No one spoke.

No one looked away.

Hagar felt exposed. Ashamed. Vulnerable in the particular way you feel when the thing you have been carrying privately is suddenly visible to a room full of people.

A voice recording drifted through the air.

Her daughter's voice.

"Love you, Mom."

Another.

"We'll visit soon."

Another.

"Sorry, we're busy."

The words pierced her. She reached toward the memories instinctively, trying to gather them, trying to stop them, trying to tuck them back into the suitcase where they had been safely contained. But more emerged. Missed phone calls. Empty holidays. Lonely birthdays. The long years of quiet abandonment she had hidden beneath her smile and her competence and her careful insistence that she was fine.

Tears spilled down her face.

"I don't want them to see this," she said. The words escaped before she could stop them.

A gentle voice answered.

"They already do."

Hagar looked up.

Elizabeth sat beside her. The older woman held her wooden box tightly in both hands, but her eyes were fixed on Hagar with an expression of such clear understanding that it stopped the breath.

Not pity.

Understanding.

The kind that comes from having carried your own version of the same thing.

"I know what it's like," Elizabeth said quietly, "to carry disappointment."

The words broke something inside Hagar. Something she had been holding together with precision and effort and the quiet determination not to let anyone see the seams.

For years she had believed she was alone in this. For years she had believed that her particular wound, the specific shape of her abandonment, and the exact texture of her loneliness were hers alone, too particular to be understood by anyone who had not lived it exactly as she had.

Then Leah moved to sit beside her.

"So do I," Leah said.

Abigail joined them.

"And me."

Soon other women gathered around. Not in a rush. Not with advice or reassurance or the particular urgency of people who need to fix what is broken. Simply staying. Moving close. Remaining present.

No judgment. No sermons. No solutions offered before the wound had been allowed to breathe.

Just presence.

For the first time in longer than she could measure, Hagar was not carrying rejection by herself.

The Driver watched quietly from the front of the bus.

A smile touched His face.

Relationships were beginning. Walls were cracking. Truth was doing what truth does when it is finally given room, moving, shifting, making space for something better.

Then something else rose from the suitcase.

A small mirror.

Unlike Rachel's mirrors, this one contained only a single reflection. Hagar's. She stared into it. The woman looking back appeared tired. Lonely. Forgotten. The face of someone who had been waiting to be returned to for so long that she had begun to wonder if the waiting itself was the answer.

The reflection whispered.

"No one wants you."

Hagar immediately looked away.

The words hurt because part of her still believed them. Not the whole of her. Not the part that had boarded the bus, not the part that had opened the suitcase. But the old part. The part that had been listening to the lie for so long that it had started to sound like wisdom.

The mirror continued.

"Your husband left. Your children left. You are alone."

Hagar's hands trembled. The lie sounded so familiar. So convincing. The kind of familiarity that feels like truth simply because it has been present for so long.

Then another voice interrupted.

Stronger. Gentler. True.

The Driver.

"Hagar."

She looked toward Him. The entire bus seemed to fall away. The other women, the scattered memories, the floating photographs, all of it receded until there was only His voice and the question He was asking.

"What did I call you when you were in the wilderness?"

The question moved through her like water through dry ground.

She remembered.

The desert. The thirst. The loneliness so complete it had felt like its own kind of death. And then the voice. Not distant. Not general. Specific. Personal. Aimed directly at her with the precision of someone who had been watching all along.

I see you.

> *"Then she called the name of the Lord who spoke to her, You-Are-the-God-Who-Sees; for she said, 'Have I also here seen Him who sees me?'"*
> — Genesis 16:13 (NKJV)

The mirror cracked.

A thin fracture appeared across its surface. Then another. Then another spreading outward from the center like ice giving way, like something that had held its shape under pressure finally releasing.

The lie was losing its power.

Tears streamed down Hagar's face. The women around her remained close. Elizabeth placed a hand on her shoulder. Leah squeezed her hand. Abigail sat beside her. Not one of them moved away. Not one of them left.

For the first time in years, Hagar allowed herself to believe something different.

Maybe abandonment was not her identity. Maybe loneliness was not her destiny. Maybe the people who left did not determine her worth.

The cracked mirror fell back into the suitcase. The lid slowly closed. Not locked. Not gone. But quieter. The burden remained. She was not pretending otherwise. But somehow it felt lighter. As though the weight of it had been redistributed among the women who had gathered close enough to share it.

The Driver smiled.

"Good."

The women looked toward Him.

"This journey is not about pretending the wounds never existed."

His gaze moved across the bus. Unhurried, taking each woman in.

"It is about discovering they do not define you."

Then Elizabeth, who had been sitting quietly beside Hagar with her wooden box in her lap, shifted slightly.

She had not opened the box.

Not yet.

But she held it differently now. Less tightly. Her knuckles were no longer white. Her shoulders had dropped from around her ears. She looked at the box the way a woman looks at something she has carried so long she forgot it was heavy. With a kind of exhausted recognition, as though she were seeing the weight for the first time now that she had seen someone else set theirs down.

"I prayed for years," she said quietly.

No one asked her to explain. They already understood. They had all prayed for things that did not come when they asked. They had all waited in silences that felt like answers they didn't want.

Elizabeth continued.

"I thought the waiting meant He wasn't listening."

She paused. Her eyes moved to the window, to the wildflowers bending in the breeze outside.

"But He was."

A tear slipped down her cheek.

"He was just preparing something I couldn't have held any earlier."

The bus was very still.

> *"But those who wait on the Lord shall renew their strength; they shall mount up with wings like eagles, they shall run and not be weary, they shall walk and not faint."* — Isaiah 40:31 (NKJV)

Abigail reached over and placed her hand on top of Elizabeth's.

No words. Just presence. The same gift she had spent her whole life giving to everyone else. Steadily, practically, without drama or announcement. Only this time, she was not managing someone else's crisis. She was not solving or strategizing or preparing a contingency plan for someone else's grief.

She was simply there.

And for the first time, being there felt like enough.

Outside, the wildflowers danced in the breeze.

Inside, something beautiful had quietly begun.

The women had boarded the bus as strangers. Each carrying her particular burden, each convinced that her wound was too specific, too private, too complicated to be understood by anyone else. But somewhere between the opening of Hagar's suitcase and the spilling of Leah's labels and Elizabeth's quiet confession about the years she had spent waiting, they were becoming something else.

Not strangers.

Not passengers.

Sisters.

The road to the Kingdom stretched on before them.

Together.

CHAPTER FOURTEEN
Baggage

Mirrors, Armor, and Maps—Rachel, Jezebel, and Rebekah

The bus had been unusually quiet since Hagar's suitcase opened.

The women sat in a thoughtful silence that was different from the silence of strangers. Heavier, more honest, the kind of quiet that settles over a room after something true has been said aloud and everyone is still deciding what to do with it. Each woman kept her eyes forward or turned toward the window, but no one was fooling anyone. They were all aware of the baggage resting beside the others. They were all aware of what had just happened. And they were all, in their own private ways, hoping the Driver would not call their name next.

Outside, the road wound through rolling hills covered in wildflowers. The light was golden and unhurried.

Inside, the atmosphere felt heavier.

More honest.

As if the opening of one suitcase—and the permission it gave everyone to stop pretending—had cracked something open in the cabin that could not quite be closed again.

The Driver guided the bus effortlessly around a long curve. Then He spoke.

"Truth has a way of making room for more truth."

Several women exchanged uneasy glances.

No one needed an explanation.

Everyone knew exactly what He meant.

The Driver smiled.

"Rachel."

Rachel immediately sat up straighter.

"What?"

The women laughed softly. The particular laughter of people who recognize themselves in someone else's reflex.

The Driver's smile widened.

"Would you open your bag?"

Rachel instinctively pulled the expensive handbag closer against her side. The mirrors inside shifted with a soft, rattling sound.

"No."

The answer came so quickly that even she seemed surprised by it.

The Driver raised an eyebrow.

"No?"

"It's private."

From across the aisle, Leah smiled. Gently, without judgment. The smile of a woman who had just watched her own labels scatter across the floor of the bus.

"We all said that."

A few women chuckled. Rachel did not. Because suddenly the bag resting on her lap felt very heavy. Much heavier than when she had boarded. The mirrors inside rattled softly, as if they were alive. Waiting. As though they had been waiting since the moment she stepped onto the bus and had simply been patient enough to let her believe she was in control.

The Driver said nothing.

He simply waited.

He was, as they were all learning, very good at waiting.

Eventually Rachel sighed.

"Fine."

She opened the bag slowly.

Immediately dozens of tiny mirrors floated into the air. Rising in a cloud around her, each one catching the light from the windows and refracting it in a dozen different directions. Gasps moved through the bus. The mirrors surrounded Rachel completely, hovering at every angle, each reflecting a different image.

A woman holding a newborn baby. A bestselling author signing books at a table lined with flowers. A family gathered around a holiday table, laughing. A successful ministry. A beautiful wedding. A larger home. A better career. A happier life.

At least that was how it appeared. That was how the mirrors always made things appear.

Rachel stared at the images. Her stomach tightened. She recognized every one of them. She had seen them before. Not in a bus, not floating in the air, but on a screen. Scrolling past in the small hours of the morning when she couldn't sleep and the house was quiet and the hunger she couldn't name had driven her to her phone again.

The mirrors began whispering.

"Look at her. She has what you want. You're falling behind. Everyone else is ahead."

The voices echoed through the cabin. Rachel covered her ears.

"Stop."

The mirrors ignored her.

"You should be further along. You deserve more. You'll never be enough."

Tears filled Rachel's eyes. For years she had lived with those voices. Scrolling. Comparing. Measuring herself against images that had been curated specifically to make her feel the lack. Competing in a race she had never agreed to enter, against women she had never met, for a finish line that kept moving.

Never realizing, until now, how much they controlled her.

> *"A sound heart is life to the body, But envy is rottenness to the bones."*
> — Proverbs 14:30 (NKJV)

Leah sat quietly beside her sister. She watched Rachel's face. The tightening jaw, the careful composure beginning to crack, the tears Rachel fought to keep hidden. Leah recognized the look immediately. Not because she had seen it in Rachel before, but because she had worn that same expression herself. It was the face of someone exhausted from carrying an identity that no longer fit.

Leah stood.

Rachel braced herself. Their relationship had carried its own particular weight for as long as either of them could remember. The complicated architecture of two sisters who had loved each other and wounded each other and measured themselves against each other in ways neither of them had ever fully named aloud.

But Leah's voice, when she spoke, was not sharp. It was not triumphant. It was simply honest.

"You know what's strange?"

Rachel looked up.

Leah smiled. A small, sad smile. The kind that carries something real.

"I spent my life wishing I looked like you."

The words stunned the bus into silence.

Rachel blinked.

"What?"

Leah laughed softly. Not at Rachel. At the absurdity of it. At the years they had both spent.

"And I think you've spent your life wishing you had what I have."

The mirrors froze.

For a moment, neither woman spoke. The bus was very still. Outside, the wildflowers moved in the breeze. Inside, something had shifted. Something that had been fixed in place between these two women for longer than either of them could remember.

Then one mirror shattered.

A single clean break. A single lie exposed. A single comparison broken at its root.

The remaining mirrors trembled. Not gone. But weakened. Stripped of some of the authority they had held for years.

The two sisters looked at each other.

Two women. Two wounds. Two people who had spent their entire lives measuring themselves against each other—and neither one had won. Neither one had ever been at peace. They had both been losing the same race from opposite sides.

Leah sat down slowly.

Rachel's hands trembled.

Before she realized what she was doing, Leah reached over and gently covered them with her own.

Rachel looked down.

Then up.

Their eyes met.

Neither sister spoke.

They no longer needed to.

Years of comparison were giving way to something they had almost forgotten was possible.

Grace.

No words passed between them. None were needed. The mirrors still floated in the air, but they had lost something. Their voices had quieted. Their reflections had dimmed. Because the comparison only worked when the two women were separated. And they were not separated anymore.

They were sisters.

Sitting shoulder to shoulder.

Not because life had finally become fair.

Not because every wound had healed.

But because they had finally stopped asking who had been loved more.

The race was over.

There was room for both daughters in the Father's house.

Rachel quietly whispered, "I didn't know."

Leah looked at her.

Rachel continued.

"I didn't know how much it hurt."

Leah simply squeezed her hand.

Not forgiveness.

Not resolution.

Just…

the beginning.

The same way Rachel had chosen to sit beside Leah on the bus. The same way Leah had quietly pressed "like" on a Tuesday afternoon and put the phone face down on top of the laundry. The same way two women who had been set against each other by circumstance and wound and the long human habit of comparison were choosing, here, on this bus, on this road, to be something else.

> *"Now godliness with contentment is great gain."* — 1 Timothy 6:6 (NKJV)

The Driver nodded.

Then His gaze shifted.

"Jezebel."

The temperature inside the bus seemed to drop by several degrees.

Jezebel sat motionless. Her black armor gleamed in the light from the windows, polished, impenetrable, sealed at every joint. She had worn it so long it had become indistinguishable from her. She already knew what was coming.

"No."

The answer was firm. Final. The kind of no that has been practiced.

The Driver's expression remained calm.

"Open it."

Jezebel crossed her arms. The armor immediately tightened around her shoulders. Metal groaned. Locks clicked. The women exchanged nervous glances.

Finally, Abigail spoke.

"Maybe you should."

Jezebel laughed. A cold sound. The kind of laugh that is not really laughter.

"Easy for you to say."

Silence followed. The kind that waits.

Then something unexpected happened.

The armor cracked.

A small fracture appeared across the chest plate, thin as a hairline, barely visible. Jezebel froze. Another crack followed, branching from the first. Then another. The women stared. The armor was opening from the inside, not forced, not broken, but releasing. As though something inside it had finally exhaled.

The armor opened.

And inside there was no strength. No confidence. No power. None of the things the armor had been built to project.

Only wounds.

Childhood memories emerged.

A father who demanded perfection and withheld approval like currency. Friends who had smiled to her face and betrayed her behind her back. A fiancé who had walked away without explanation. A business partner who had stolen from her and then acted as though she were the one who had done something wrong.

One betrayal after another. One heartbreak after another. One person after another who had gotten close enough to hurt her and then done exactly that.

The bus grew silent.

Even Hagar's eyes filled with compassion. Because suddenly they all understood. Not the Jezebel they had assumed, the one who controlled and manipulated and kept everyone at a calculated distance. But the one underneath. The one who had built the armor because the alternative, staying open, staying soft, staying reachable, had cost her too much, too many times.

Jezebel hadn't built armor because she was cruel.

She had built armor because she was afraid.

A small voice emerged from inside the armor. Young. Broken. Terrified. The voice of a girl who had learned the lesson too early and too hard.

"If I let people close, they'll leave."

The words fell into the silence of the bus like a stone into still water.

No one laughed. No one judged. No one offered a quick correction or a cheerful reassurance.

Because every woman on that bus understood what it meant to build walls around a wound. They had all done it in their own ways, with their own materials. Labels and mirrors and planners and armor and clay jars and velvet garment bags. Different shapes. Same function. Same fear underneath.

> *"There is no fear in love; but perfect love casts out fear, because fear involves torment. But he who fears has not been made perfect in love."*—
> 1 John 4:18 (NKJV)

Jezebel immediately tried to close the armor.

But it was too late.

The truth was already visible. Already in the room. Already seen by twelve women who were not looking at her with judgment but with the particular recognition of people who have seen something of themselves in someone they expected to be nothing like them.

The Driver spoke gently.

"The armor protected you."

Jezebel looked away.

"It also imprisoned you."

The words landed heavily. Jezebel had no argument for them. No defense prepared. Only silence—and in the silence, something she had not felt in a very long time.

The first small crack of recognition.

That what she called strength had been exhausting her for years. That the armor was heavy. That she had been so busy maintaining it she had forgotten what it felt like to breathe without it.

She sat very still.

The armor remained on her shoulders. She was not ready to remove it. Not yet. Not entirely. But something inside it had shifted. Something had heard the truth and could not quite unhear it.

That was enough for now.

The Driver knew it.

"Rebekah."

Rebekah looked down at the planner resting in her lap. The leather cover trembled. Before she could react—before she could flip to a page, or locate a plan, or devise a strategy for what was about to happen—it opened.

Pages flew through the air.

Maps. Schedules. Emergency plans. Backup plans. Backup plans for the backup plans. Contingency strategies for outcomes she had not yet experienced but had already prepared for.

The women stared. The sheer volume was astonishing. Pages floated through the cabin like leaves in the wind, each one covered in Rebekah's careful handwriting.

One page drifted toward Abigail.

She read aloud.

"Plan for if Daniel moves."

Another.

"Plan for if Daniel fails."

Another.

"Plan for if Daniel succeeds."

The bus erupted in laughter—genuine, warm, the laughter of recognition. Even Rebekah laughed, embarrassed and relieved at once.

The pages continued.

Plan for church. Plan for family. Plan for retirement. Plan for health. Plan for grief. Plan for uncertainty. Plan for everything that might go wrong and several things that probably wouldn't.

Then the final page appeared.

Unlike the others, it was not covered in Rebekah's handwriting. Unlike the others, it was not color-coded or cross-referenced or annotated in the margins. It contained only one sentence, written in gold ink in a hand she did not recognize.

What happens if you trust Me?

The laughter stopped.

The page hovered in front of Rebekah. She stared at it. Her eyes filled with tears. Not the sudden, surprised tears of someone caught off guard, but the slow, inevitable tears of someone who has known for a long time that a question was coming and had spent years avoiding the answer.

Because despite all her planning—despite the color-coded tabs and the contingency strategies and the years of careful preparation—she had never truly answered the question.

She had planned around God. She had planned beside God. She had even planned for God.

But she had never simply trusted Him.

> *"Trust in the Lord with all your heart, and lean not on your own understanding; in all your ways acknowledge Him, and He shall direct your paths." — Proverbs 3:5–6 (NKJV)*

The page drifted slowly into her lap.

Rebekah held it carefully. As though it might dissolve. As though she might dissolve.

"I didn't trust Him," she said quietly.

No one rushed to correct her. No one offered reassurance. No one said *of course you did* or *don't be so hard on yourself.* The truth deserved a moment to breathe.

"I thought if I planned well enough, I could protect everyone."

She paused.

"But I was really just protecting myself."

From uncertainty. From loss. From the terrifying possibility that the outcome might not be in her hands, that she might do everything right and still not be able to prevent the thing she feared most. That she might have to trust Someone else with the people she loved most.

The Driver nodded.

Gently.

Knowingly.

"That is why you are here."

The bus grew quiet.

Three women. Three burdens. Three wounds.

Rachel carried comparison. The endless, exhausting measurement of her life against the lives of others, the hunger that could not be filled by anything the mirrors showed her.

Jezebel carried self-protection. The armor built so carefully, maintained so vigilantly, that she had forgotten what it felt like to be known.

Rebekah carried control. The planner full of contingency plans, the life organized against uncertainty, the deep and private terror of what might happen if she simply let go.

Different baggage.

Same fear.

The fear that God might not be enough. The fear that they would have to be.

The realization settled over the group slowly, the way morning settles. Not arriving all at once, but accumulating, brightening, until the darkness has simply receded without anyone marking the exact moment it went.

Then something remarkable happened.

Hagar stood.

The woman who had once believed she was forgotten. The woman whose suitcase had opened first, whose memories had floated through the bus like an accusation, whose mirror had whispered the lie she had been carrying for years. The woman who had wept on the floor of her own story and been gathered by women who stayed.

She walked toward Rachel.

Then Jezebel.

Then Rebekah.

And placed a hand on each of their shoulders.

Not advice. Not a sermon. Not a correction or a solution or a plan for moving forward. Just presence. The same gift the others had given her. Returned now, without ceremony, because that is what you do when someone has carried you. You carry them back.

One by one the remaining women joined them.

Leah. Abigail. Elizabeth. Mary Magdalene. Priscilla. The Woman at the Well. Bathsheba. Lot's Wife.

Soon a circle had formed around the three women. Not perfectly. Not with any particular order or choreography. Just women moving toward other women the way people move toward warmth when they have been cold.

The baggage remained open.

The wounds remained visible.

But none of them stood alone.

The Driver watched from the front of the bus.

A smile touched His face. The kind of smile that belongs to someone who has been waiting for exactly this moment and is not surprised that it arrived, only glad.

Relationships were forming. Walls were falling. Truth was doing its work.

Outside, the road stretched toward the horizon. Long and golden and impossibly clear. Inside, three women had begun confronting the lies they had carried for years. The journey was becoming harder.

But it was also becoming holy.

> *"Confess your trespasses to one another, and pray for one another, that you may be healed." — James 5:16 (NKJV)*

And somewhere ahead, the Kingdom waited.

Patient. Certain. Ready.

CHAPTER FIFTEEN
Baggage

The Weight of Yesterday—Lot's Wife and Bathsheba

The bus traveled beneath a sky washed in silver and gold.

Clouds drifted lazily overhead, casting moving shadows across the countryside. Endless fields stretched toward the horizon, interrupted only by winding streams that sparkled beneath the afternoon sun.

Inside the bus, however, the atmosphere felt heavier than the day before.

The women had begun opening their baggage.

And once truth was revealed, it could never be hidden again.

The Driver sat quietly at the front, His hands steady on the wheel.

He didn't rush them.

He never did.

Healing moved at the speed of honesty.

And honesty was arriving one suitcase at a time.

Lot's Wife sat near the window, her weathered memory box resting beside her.

Since the previous day's revelations, she hadn't touched it.

Hadn't opened it.

Hadn't even looked at it.

Yet she could feel it there.

Waiting.

The box seemed heavier than before.

As if the memories inside had become aware they were losing their hold on her.

Across the aisle, Bathsheba stared at her garment bag.

The labels were gone.

The accusations had disappeared.

But the crown remained.

Resting quietly inside.

Waiting.

Neither woman knew what to do with what had been revealed.

The truth had surfaced.

The wounds were visible.

Yet healing still felt uncertain.

Like standing at the edge of a river, you knew you needed to cross but couldn't yet bring yourself to enter.

The bus rounded a curve.

The Driver slowed.

Then, unexpectedly, He pulled onto a narrow road lined with towering trees.

Their branches arched overhead like the vaulted ceiling of a cathedral.

The women looked around.

Something was different.

The landscape itself seemed to hold its breath.

The bus came to a gentle stop.

Silence settled over the cabin.

Then the Driver stood.

His eyes moved across the women before resting on Lot's Wife and Bathsheba.

"Today," He said softly, "we go deeper."

A nervous laugh escaped Rachel.

"I was afraid You were going to say that."

Several women smiled.

The Driver chuckled.

Then His gaze returned to the two women.

"Open them again."

Lot's Wife immediately shook her head.

"No."

Bathsheba wasn't far behind.

"I think we already did this."

The Driver smiled.

"No."

His voice remained gentle.

"You opened the wound."

He paused.

"Today we discover what created it."

The bus grew quiet.

Neither woman moved.

Then Elizabeth spoke softly from behind them.

"I'll go first if it helps."

She placed a comforting hand on Lot's Wife's shoulder.

The gesture wasn't dramatic.

Just supportive.

A reminder that none of them were alone.

Lot's Wife inhaled slowly.

Then opened the box.

At first nothing happened.

Then the photographs returned.

The same smiling faces.

The same successful moments.

The same carefully preserved memories.

But this time the images moved differently.

Instead of floating through the air, they began replaying like scenes from a film.

The women watched.

Lot's Wife saw herself standing in a beautiful kitchen.

Guests filled the house.

Everyone laughed.

Everything appeared perfect.

Then the scene widened.

The smile faded.

The laughter ended.

The guests left.

And there she was.

Alone.

Standing in silence.

The image changed.

A business award ceremony.

Applause.

Recognition.

Success.

Again, the picture widened.

Again, the truth appeared.

Exhaustion.

Anxiety.

Fear.

Pressure.

The illusion shattered.

One memory after another revealed the same pattern.

The life she missed had not been nearly as perfect as she remembered.

She had been curating the highlight reel.

And somewhere along the way, she had mistaken the reel for real life.

Finally, Lot's Wife whispered the truth she had avoided for years.

"I don't miss the life."

The women looked at her.

Tears filled her eyes.

"I miss who I thought I was."

The confession settled over the bus.

Heavy.

Honest.

Painful.

The memory box trembled.

A crack appeared along one side.

Then another.

The Driver nodded.

"Now we're getting somewhere."

Lot's Wife laughed through her tears.

The sound surprised her.

Because for the first time she wasn't defending the past.

She was grieving it.

And grief was healthier than denial.

> *"Do not remember the former things, nor consider the things of old. Behold, I will do a new thing; now it shall spring forth. Shall you not know it? I will even make a road in the wilderness and rivers in the desert." — Isaiah 43:18–19 (NKJV)*

She looked out the window.

The narrow road stretched ahead through the trees.

A road where there had been none.

She had not noticed it until now.

She had been too busy looking back.

The crack in the memory box widened.

Not breaking.

Breathing.

As if the box itself needed to exhale.

Beside her, Bathsheba slowly reached for her garment bag.

The zipper opened.

The crown emerged once more.

Golden.

Radiant.

Beautiful.

Yet something else followed.

A mirror.

The sight stole her breath.

She had never seen it before.

The mirror floated above her lap.

At first, it reflected the woman she knew.

The successful executive.

The composed professional.

The survivor.

Then the reflection shifted.

Suddenly she was younger.

Terrified.

Humiliated.

Broken.

The version of herself that emerged after the scandal.

The woman she spent years trying to bury.

The woman she hoped nobody remembered.

The mirror spoke.

Not aloud.

Inside her heart.

"You should have known better."

The words cut deeply.

"You ruined everything."

Bathsheba lowered her eyes.

Because she still believed it.

Part of her always would.

The mirror continued.

"You don't deserve redemption."

Before Bathsheba could respond, another voice interrupted.

The Woman at the Well.

"No."

The bus grew still.

Everyone turned.

The Woman at the Well leaned forward.

Tears filled her eyes.

"No."

She repeated it.

Stronger this time.

"I know that voice."

Bathsheba looked at her.

The Woman at the Well smiled sadly.

"It used to speak to me every day."

Silence settled over the bus.

The connection formed instantly.

Two women.

Different stories.

The same shame.

The same lies.

The Woman at the Well continued.

"It keeps telling you who you were."

She nodded toward the mirror.

"But God keeps telling you who you are."

The mirror trembled.

A crack spread slowly across its surface.

Before anyone could speak again, Rachel's quiet voice broke the silence.

"I know that voice too."

Every eye turned toward her.

Rachel wasn't looking at Bathsheba.

She was looking down at her own hands, folded tightly in her lap.

"The words were different."

She swallowed.

"But the lies were the same."

Leah slipped her hand gently over Rachel's.

Rachel didn't pull away.

"The mirrors kept telling me I'd never have enough."

She laughed softly through gathering tears.

"More success."

"More recognition."

"More followers."

"More."

"They convinced me contentment was always one blessing away."

She looked toward Bathsheba.

"Your mirror tells you you're condemned."

She glanced toward the shattered mirrors that had once surrounded her.

"Mine told me I'd never arrive."

She smiled sadly.

"But neither one was telling the truth."

Leah squeezed her hand.

Then, for the first time since boarding the bus, Rachel turned fully toward her sister.

"I didn't know."

The words were barely above a whisper.

Leah looked at her.

Rachel's eyes filled.

"I didn't know how much it hurt you."

Silence.

Not awkward.

Holy.

"I thought…"

Rachel's voice trembled.

"I thought because you smiled… because you kept showing up… because you never complained… that you were okay."

Leah's own eyes glistened.

"I wasn't."

Rachel nodded slowly.

"I know."

Another crack spread across Bathsheba's mirror.

Mary Magdalene stood.

"I know that voice too."

Another crack.

Hagar stood.

"So do I."

Another.

Priscilla.

Elizabeth.

Lot's Wife.

One by one, the women began speaking. Not sermons, not advice, but testimony.

Each confession weakened the mirror.

Each truth stole another lie's authority.

Until finally Bathsheba realized something.

She wasn't the only broken woman on the bus.

She wasn't even the most broken.

And somehow that truth felt freeing.

> *"For all have sinned and fall short of the glory of God, being justified freely by His grace through the redemption that is in Christ Jesus."* — Romans 3:23–24 (NKJV)

The mirror shattered.

The sound echoed through the cabin.

Tiny fragments dissolved into light.

Only the crown remained.

Bathsheba reached toward it.

For the first time.

The moment her fingers touched it, tears spilled down her face.

Not because she felt worthy.

Because she was finally beginning to believe redemption was possible.

> *"He has not dealt with us according to our sins, nor punished us according to our iniquities. For as the heavens are high above the earth, so great is His mercy toward those who fear Him; as far as the east is from the west, so far has He removed our transgressions from us." — Psalm 103:10–12 (NKJV)*

The Driver smiled.

Then He looked at both women.

Lot's Wife.

Bathsheba.

One trapped by longing.

One trapped by shame.

Both trapped by yesterday.

The Driver's voice filled the bus.

"The enemy wants your identity attached to your past."

The women listened.

"I want your identity attached to Me."

Silence followed.

Holy silence.

Healing silence.

The kind of silence that arrives after truth has finally been spoken aloud and no one has run from it.

Lot's Wife closed the memory box.

She did not slam it.

She did not force it.

She simply *closed it.*

Gently.

The way you close a chapter you have finally finished reading.

Bathsheba placed the crown back inside the garment bag.

Her hands were steadier than before.

Neither burden had disappeared.

Not yet.

But something had changed.

The burdens no longer owned them.

Outside, the sun broke through the clouds.

Golden light poured across the road ahead.

The Driver returned to His seat.

The engine hummed softly.

The bus began moving once more.

The narrow road through the trees opened gradually into a wide, sunlit valley.

The women exhaled.

As if the landscape itself had given them permission to breathe.

> *"Therefore, if anyone is in Christ, he is a new creation; old things have passed away; behold, all things have become new." — 2 Corinthians 5:17 (NKJV)*

And as the Kingdom drew closer, two more women discovered that freedom wasn't found by forgetting the past.

Freedom was found by allowing God to redeem it.

The journey continued.

And for the first time, both women found themselves looking less toward yesterday, *and more toward the promise waiting ahead.*

CHAPTER SIXTEEN
Baggage

Empty Jars, Heavy Shawls, and Forgotten Names—Woman at the Well, Priscilla, and Mary Magdalene

The bus traveled through a landscape unlike any the women had seen before.

Outside the windows, vast fields of wildflowers stretched toward distant hills bathed in golden light. Streams wound through the valleys like ribbons of silver, and the sky seemed impossibly wide.

The beauty should have felt peaceful.

Instead, a quiet tension lingered inside the bus.

The women had learned something important over the past few days.

Every suitcase carried a story.

Every burden hid a wound.

And every wound concealed a lie.

The Driver continued down the road, saying very little.

He didn't need to.

The baggage was beginning to speak for itself.

Near the middle of the bus, the Woman at the Well sat with her cracked water jar resting in her lap.

Across from her, Priscilla adjusted the heavy gray shawl wrapped around her shoulders.

A few rows ahead, Mary Magdalene stared at the collection of volunteer badges hanging from her shoulder.

Three women.

Three burdens.

Three different kinds of thirst.

The Driver glanced into the rearview mirror.

Then He smiled.

"The next three."

Immediately the women froze.

Rachel groaned.

"Oh, somebody's about to get exposed."

Rachel laughed at first.

Then she glanced toward Leah.

Leah was smiling too.

The smile surprised Rachel.

For years she had been so busy watching herself that she had forgotten how beautiful her sister looked when she laughed.

Without thinking, Rachel leaned lightly against Leah's shoulder.

Leah didn't move.

She simply smiled and looked toward the Driver.

Somehow the bus already felt more like home.

Laughter rippled through the bus.

The Driver chuckled.

"The Woman at the Well."

The laughter disappeared.

The Woman at the Well lowered her eyes.

Her fingers tightened around the clay jar.

She already knew what was coming.

The jar trembled.

Then cracked.

A thin fracture spread across its surface.

Another followed.

Then another.

Without warning, the jar burst open.

The women gasped.

Instead of water, memories poured out.

Conversations.

Relationships.

Promises.

Faces.

One after another.

A high school sweetheart.

A fiancé who left.

A boyfriend who cheated.

A man who only called when he was lonely.

Another who wanted her body but not her heart.

Another who promised forever and disappeared.

The memories swirled through the bus like drifting smoke.

The Woman at the Well closed her eyes.

She couldn't bear to watch.

The whispers came next.

Not from the memories.

From the jar itself.

"You'll always be alone."

The words struck hard.

"You are too much."

Another whisper.

"You are not enough."

The women sat silently.

Because every one of them knew those voices.

They had all heard them.

In different rooms.

In different seasons.

Wearing different faces.

But the same voice.

The Woman at the Well finally spoke.

"So many times…"

Her voice cracked.

"So many times I thought the next person would fix what was broken."

The confession hung in the air.

Raw.

Painful.

Honest.

"I kept looking for love in people who couldn't give me what only God could."

Leah quietly whispered, "I looked for it in one person's eyes."

Rachel answered softly, "I looked for it in everyone's."

> *"Jesus answered and said to her, 'Whoever drinks of this water will thirst again, but whoever drinks of the water that I shall give him will never thirst. But the water that I shall give him will become in him a fountain of water springing up into everlasting life.'"* — John 4:13–14 (NKJV)

Silence followed.

Then Hagar stood.

The Woman at the Well looked up.

Hagar smiled gently.

"I know what it's like to want someone to stay."

The words settled softly.

Not judgment.

Understanding.

Then Bathsheba spoke.

"I know what it's like to let loneliness convince you to make decisions you regret."

Rachel looked at the broken jar.

"I spent years believing the next achievement would satisfy me."

She smiled sadly.

"Different thirst. Same emptiness."

The Woman at the Well's eyes filled with tears.

For years she had carried shame.

Now she discovered something unexpected.

She wasn't alone.

The jar trembled.

Then another crack appeared.

A lie was losing its power.

The Driver nodded.

Then His gaze shifted.

"Priscilla."

The heavy shawl tightened immediately.

The embroidered words seemed to darken.

Stay Quiet.

Don't Make Waves.

Keep Everyone Happy.

Priscilla swallowed hard.

"No."

The answer came automatically.

A response she had practiced for most of her life.

The Driver smiled.

"Exactly."

The women looked confused.

Priscilla looked confused.

The Driver pointed toward the shawl.

"Open it."

Slowly Priscilla loosened the fabric.

The shawl unfolded.

And memories spilled out.

A young bride.

A nervous smile.

A woman constantly apologizing.

Constantly adjusting.

Constantly shrinking.

The women watched as scene after scene played before them.

Priscilla giving up opportunities.

Giving up dreams.

Giving up opinions.

Giving up herself.

Every memory carried the same message.

Be less.

Take up less space.

Need less.

Speak less.

The sight broke something in Leah.

"No."

The word escaped before she could stop it.

Priscilla looked up.

Leah shook her head.

"That's not submission."

Leah's voice trembled.

"That's disappearing."

She looked toward Rachel.

"God never asked either of us to become less so someone else could become more."

Rachel quietly nodded.

No dialogue.

Just tears.

The bus grew quiet.

Priscilla's eyes widened.

The words pierced deeply.

Because she had spent years confusing obedience with erasure.

Confusing peace with silence.

Confusing love with disappearing.

Then Abigail stood.

Her voice remained calm.

"Godly submission doesn't require you to disappear."

The shawl trembled.

Several embroidered words began fading.

> *"For we are His workmanship, created in Christ Jesus for good works, which God prepared beforehand that we should walk in them."* — Ephesians 2:10 (NKJV)

Another woman rose.

Mary Magdalene.

"You know what I see?"

Priscilla wiped her eyes.

"What?"

"A woman who survived."

The answer stunned her.

For years she had viewed herself as weak.

Broken.

Passive.

Mary smiled.

"I see courage."

More words vanished from the shawl.

The fabric seemed lighter.

Not gone.

But lighter.

For the first time, Priscilla wondered if strength and gentleness could coexist.

If a woman could be both soft and powerful.

Both yielded and whole.

Both submitted and fully herself.

She looked down at the shawl.

The words that remained were fading.

Not because she was removing them.

Because truth was replacing them.

Then the Driver spoke again.

"Mary."

Mary Magdalene froze.

The volunteer badges rattled softly.

She sighed.

"I knew this was coming."

The women laughed.

Even Mary smiled.

Then the badges began slipping loose.

One by one they floated into the air.

Teacher.

Volunteer.

Leader.

Coordinator.

Helper.

Servant.

The titles filled the bus.

Dozens of them.

Hundreds.

The women stared.

Mary looked embarrassed.

"I may have overcommitted."

The bus erupted in laughter.

Even the Driver smiled.

Then something unexpected happened.

A final badge appeared.

Different from the others.

Larger.

Heavier.

It read:

VALUED

Mary's smile disappeared.

The women looked confused.

The Driver wasn't.

He understood immediately.

Mary lowered her eyes.

Tears filled them.

For years she had served faithfully.

But beneath the service hid a secret.

A painful one.

She wasn't serving because she felt loved.

She was serving because she hoped to become lovable.

The realization devastated her.

"If I stop helping…"

Her voice cracked.

"If I stop serving…"

Silence filled the bus.

The Driver finished the sentence.

"You think people won't see you."

Mary nodded.

The truth finally exposed.

Years of striving.

Years of proving.

Years of earning.

> *"But God demonstrates His own love toward us, in that while we were still sinners, Christ died for us." — Romans 5:8 (NKJV)*

He did not wait until she earned it.

He did not love her because of the badges.

He loved her before she picked up a single one.

Then Elizabeth stood.

The older woman smiled warmly.

"Mary."

She looked up.

"I saw you before the badges."

Tears immediately spilled down Mary's cheeks.

One by one the women nodded.

Hagar.

Leah.

Priscilla.

Bathsheba.

Abigail.

The Woman at the Well.

Rachel paused. "You never had to earn your seat beside me."

Mary looked confused.

Rachel smiled.

"I've been learning that myself."

Every one of them. *They saw her.* Not her service.

Her.

The badges began dissolving.

Not because service was wrong.

Because it was never supposed to be her identity.

The final badge disappeared.

VALUED

Gone.

But something remained in its place.

Not a badge.

Not a title.

A name.

Written not on fabric or metal.

But on her heart.

Beloved.

> *"Fear not, for I have redeemed you; I have called you by your name; you are Mine." — Isaiah 43:1 (NKJV)*

The Driver smiled.

Then He spoke to all three women.

The Woman at the Well.

Priscilla.

Mary Magdalene.

"You have spent your lives searching for worth."

The bus grew silent.

"In relationships."

His eyes moved to the broken jar.

"In approval."

His gaze shifted to the fading shawl.

"In service."

His attention settled on the dissolving badges.

The Driver's voice softened.

"But your worth was never lost."

Tears flowed freely now.

Across the bus.

Across the aisle.

Across wounded hearts.

The women slowly moved closer.

Not because they had all lived the same story.

But because they finally understood they were all fighting the same battle.

The battle to believe they were already loved.

Already seen.

Already chosen.

> *"Behold what manner of love the Father has bestowed on us, that we should be called children of God! Therefore the world does not know us, because it did not know Him."* — *1 John 3:1 (NKJV)*

The road stretched endlessly ahead.

The Kingdom still waited in the distance.

But something beautiful was happening long before they reached the gates.

The women were becoming sisters. Not because they shared the same stories, but because they were finally carrying one another's burden.

Leah looked at Rachel.

Rachel smiled back.

Somewhere along the road, comparison had quietly surrendered to compassion.

Neither sister had noticed the exact moment it happened.

They only knew they no longer wanted to make this journey without the other.

The Driver saw it in the mirror.

He smiled.

This was why He had brought them together.

And for the first time, their baggage was no longer something they carried alone.

The Driver looked into the rearview mirror one final time.

Every seat was full.

Every woman present.

Every wound exposed.

Every heart a little more open than before.

He smiled.

And kept driving.

CHAPTER SEVENTEEN

The Driver Teaches

The bus had been moving for what felt like hours. No one had spoken in a long time. The women sat with their opened burdens in their laps, or at their feet, or pressed against their chests. Outside, the landscape had changed. No one could say exactly when.

The road stretched endlessly before them.

Morning sunlight poured across the hills beyond the windows, turning the fields outside into oceans of gold. Wildflowers swayed in the breeze. Streams glittered beneath the light.

The landscape was beautiful.

Yet inside the bus, beauty felt far away.

No one spoke.

The women sat surrounded by the evidence of their own hearts.

Suitcases rested beside seats.

Memory boxes remained closed.

The planner sat on Rebekah's lap.

The crown remained hidden inside Bathsheba's garment bag.

Rachel's mirrors were silent.

Jezebel's armor reflected the sunlight like polished steel.

The silence wasn't peaceful.

It was the silence that follows exposure.

The silence that follows truth.

Healing, it turned out, was exhausting.

Hagar rested her forehead against the window.

The glass felt cool against skin still swollen from tears shed over the past several days.

She thought she would feel better after opening her suitcase.

Instead, she felt raw.

As if someone had peeled away a layer she had spent years using for protection.

Leah sat quietly beside Rachel, her fingers tracing the faded labels that still clung to her leather bag. Rachel noticed the movement immediately. A few days earlier she wouldn't have. Now she couldn't seem to stop watching her sister. Healing had given her new eyes.

The bus continued forward.

The Driver said nothing.

The women said nothing.

Finally, Abigail broke the silence.

"I thought we'd be farther along by now."

Several heads lifted.

Abigail laughed softly.

"Spiritually, I mean."

A few women smiled.

The Driver chuckled.

"According to whose timetable?"

Rebekah groaned.

The women laughed.

Everyone knew exactly why.

The Driver glanced at her through the mirror.

"You especially."

More laughter followed.

Even Rebekah smiled.

A little.

Then the laughter faded.

The silence returned.

Heavier this time.

Thoughtful.

Until Rebekah finally asked the question.

"Why us?"

The Driver didn't answer.

The bus continued rolling.

Rebekah sat forward.

"Seriously."

She looked around.

At Hagar.

At Bathsheba.

At Jezebel.

At herself.

"We're a mess."

No one laughed this time.

Because it was true.

The Driver remained silent.

Outside, a hawk circled above the valley.

The engine hummed softly beneath them.

The women waited.

And waited.

The silence became uncomfortable.

Then painful.

Then revealing.

Because during that silence, each woman found herself wondering the same thing.

Maybe He invited the wrong people.

The thought struck Leah unexpectedly.

Maybe I don't belong here.

Rachel looked down at her bag.

Maybe someone more deserving should be sitting in my seat.

Bathsheba felt the familiar ache of shame.

Maybe redemption was meant for women who hadn't done what I did.

Jezebel crossed her arms.

Maybe I shouldn't have boarded at all.

The Driver finally spoke.

"I invited you because you are a mess."

The women blinked.

Rachel frowned.

"That doesn't sound encouraging."

The Driver smiled.

"It is the most encouraging thing you'll hear all day."

The bus grew quiet.

The Driver continued.

"Most people believe they must become worthy before beginning the journey."

His eyes met theirs through the mirror.

"They spend their lives cleaning themselves up before coming to Me."

His smile softened.

"The Kingdom has never been filled with people who had it all together."

His gaze moved slowly across the bus.

"The Kingdom is filled with people who finally admitted they didn't."

> *"But God has chosen the foolish things of the world to put to shame the wise, and God has chosen the weak things of the world to put to shame the things which are mighty."* — 1 Corinthians 1:27 (NKJV)

Something shifted.

Subtle.

But real.

Bathsheba lowered her eyes.

The words reached places she rarely allowed anyone to touch.

The Driver continued.

"You each boarded carrying baggage."

His eyes settled on Hagar.

"**Hagar** carried rejection."

Hagar swallowed.

Even hearing the word hurt.

A familiar ache tightened in her chest.

The Driver turned.

"**Leah** carried the belief that she was never chosen."

Leah's fingers instinctively touched the remaining labels. Though many had fallen away, that lie still whispered from time to time.

Lot's Wife had not moved from her seat since boarding.

While the others opened their bags and wept and spoke, she had simply sat facing the rear window. Not literally. But in every way that mattered.

The Driver's eyes found her through the mirror.

"**Lot's Wife** carried yesterday."

She said nothing.

But her hands tightened slowly in her lap.

Outside, the road behind them had already disappeared around the bend.

There was nothing back there to return to.

She knew that.

She just hadn't stopped looking.

"**Rachel** carried the burden of never believing she had enough."

Rachel closed her eyes.

The words landed more deeply than she expected.

She had spent years chasing the next achievement, the next compliment, the next milestone, believing contentment was always just beyond her reach.

She glanced toward Leah.

For so long she had believed her sister wanted what she possessed.

Only now did she realize she had spent a lifetime overlooking what she herself already had.

The Driver continued.

"**Rebekah** carried control."

Rebekah sighed heavily.

"**Abigail** carried self-reliance."

Abigail lowered her eyes.

She had worn competence for so long that she had forgotten that it was never meant to carry the weight of her soul.

The Driver continued.

"**Priscilla** carried silence."

Priscilla looked toward the floor.

The Driver continued.

"**The Woman at the Well** carried the belief that love required something from her first."

She looked down at her hands. Every man. Every promise. Every relationship that had felt like water and turned to dust before she could drink.

She had spent her life offering pieces of herself in exchange for belonging.

She was still learning that belonging was never a transaction.

That the only One who had ever offered her water without a price had been sitting across from her at a well she almost didn't stop at.

The Driver continued.

"**Bathsheba** carried shame."

Bathsheba closed her eyes.

The word felt like a wound.

The Driver continued.

"**Jezebel** carried armor."

Jezebel's jaw tightened.

Armor sounded far less noble than strength.

Mary Magdalene had spent most of the journey refilling water cups.

Straightening things.

Making sure everyone else was comfortable before she allowed herself to feel anything at all.

The Driver caught her eye through the mirror.

"Mary."

She stopped mid-reach for someone's fallen scarf.

"Sit down."

She blinked.

"But I was just—"

"I know."

His voice was gentle.

Unmovable.

"Sit down."

She sat.

And for the first time in longer than she could remember, she let someone else tend to her.

"**Mary Magdalene** carried performance," the Driver said quietly. "The belief that love had to be earned through usefulness."

Her eyes filled.

She had never once considered that she might be allowed to simply be without doing a single thing to deserve it.

The Driver continued.

"**Elizabeth** carried disappointment."

Elizabeth's eyes immediately filled with tears.

And suddenly a memory surfaced.

A small nursery.

Yellow walls.

An empty crib.

A prayer whispered thirty years ago.

"Please, Lord."

She hadn't thought about that prayer in years.

Yet now she could hear it as clearly as if she had spoken it yesterday.

The tears came before she could stop them.

The Driver noticed.

He always noticed.

Then Hagar spoke.

Her voice was small.

Fragile.

"Why didn't You take it away?"

The question settled heavily over the bus.

Rachel quietly reached for Leah's hand.

Neither woman looked at the other.

They didn't need to.

Some questions belonged to every daughter on the bus.

Hagar looked toward Him.

Tears already gathering.

"If You knew how much it hurt…"

Her voice cracked.

No one looked away.

"If You knew how many nights I cried…"

The tears escaped now.

"If You knew how many times I begged You to make it stop…"

The bus fell silent.

Every woman felt the pain in her words.

Hagar wiped her face.

"I prayed."

Her shoulders trembled.

"I prayed until I had nothing left."

The Driver's expression softened.

Yet He didn't answer immediately.

Instead, He let her words remain.

Let them breathe.

Let them matter.

Finally, He spoke.

"Because what is given away too easily is rarely understood."

Rachel immediately sat forward.

"That doesn't seem fair."

The bus turned towards her.

She looked almost angry.

Somewhat surprised by her own courage.

"You let us carry this stuff for decades."

The Driver nodded.

"Yes."

Rachel shook her head.

"Why?"

The Driver slowed the bus slightly.

The road curved upward.

Mountains appeared in the distance.

Majestic. Impossible. Still far away.

"If I had removed your baggage before you understood it…"

His voice remained gentle.

"You would eventually pick it up again."

Silence followed.

Then He added:

"Most people do."

Rachel leaned back slowly.

For the first time she wondered if comparison had never been her greatest burden.

Perhaps certainty had been.

She had been so certain she understood herself.

So certain she understood Leah.

She had been wrong about both.

The words hit hard.

Especially for Rebekah.

Because she could already imagine herself rebuilding another planner.

Another system. Another illusion of control.

Then unexpectedly, Jezebel spoke.

"Maybe some of us didn't want it removed."

Every head turned.

The confession surprised everyone.

Including her.

Jezebel immediately looked away.

Her armor seemed to tighten around her shoulders.

The Driver remained quiet.

Waiting.

Jezebel sighed.

For a moment she looked tired.

Not intimidating.

Not powerful.

Just tired.

"If I put down the armor…"

Her voice softened.

"If I put it down, people can hurt me."

No one laughed.

No one argued.

Because suddenly the strongest woman on the bus looked frightened.

The Driver nodded.

"Yes."

The answer surprised her.

"Yes?"

"You can be hurt."

The bus grew still.

The Driver's eyes met hers.

"But you can also be loved."

Jezebel immediately looked away.

The truth unsettled her more than any accusation could.

> *"There is no fear in love; but perfect love casts out fear, because fear involves torment. But he who fears has not been made perfect in love." — 1 John 4:18 (NKJV)*

Then Leah spoke.

Quietly.

Almost to herself.

"What if the labels are true?"

The words barely reached the aisle.

Yet everyone heard them.

Leah stared at her bag.

At the remaining labels.

What if I really am second best?

The Driver stood.

Without letting go of the wheel.

Without anyone understanding how.

He walked slowly down the aisle.

Stopping beside Leah.

He knelt.

Then gently removed one label.

Not Enough.

He held it up.

"Who told you this?"

Leah opened her mouth.

Then closed it.

She honestly didn't know anymore.

The lie was older than memory.

The Driver smiled.

"Exactly."

The label dissolved into dust.

Leah wept quietly.

Rachel watched the dust disappear into the sunlight.

Then whispered,

"I believed it too."

Leah looked up.

Rachel smiled through tears.

"Mine just wore different words."

The Driver looked at both sisters.

"The enemy never needed identical lies."

He smiled gently.

"Only believable ones."

> *"For you are all sons of God through faith in Christ Jesus." — Galatians 3:26 (NKJV)*

Then Bathsheba spoke.

The words almost failed to leave her lips.

"What if He remembers?"

The bus grew still.

Everyone knew who she meant.

God.

Bathsheba's hands shook.

"What if He forgives everyone except me?"

The question broke something in the room.

Because beneath every wound lived the same fear.

Maybe grace belongs to someone else.

The Driver turned toward her.

His eyes filled with compassion.

"Bathsheba."

Her tears came instantly.

"If I wanted to condemn you…"

His voice softened.

"I would never have invited you."

The words pierced every heart on the bus.

Not just hers.

Everyone's.

Because suddenly they understood.

The invitation itself was evidence.

Evidence of grace.

Evidence of love.

Evidence that none of them had been forgotten.

> *"There is therefore now no condemnation for those who are in Christ Jesus, who do not walk according to the flesh but according to the Spirit."*
> *— Romans 8:1 (NKJV)*

The Driver returned to the front.

Then pointed toward the windshield.

"Look."

Every woman turned.

The mountains now dominated the horizon.

Golden light rested upon their peaks.

Majestic.

Beautiful.

Holy.

The sight stole their breath.

For the first time, the Kingdom felt real.

Not merely a destination.

A promise.

Elizabeth whispered a prayer.

Leah cried openly.

Hagar smiled through tears.

Even Rachel felt hope stirring.

Then the Driver spoke again.

"The road ahead will become harder."

Groans filled the bus.

Rachel threw up her hands.

"Of course it will."

Laughter erupted.

Even the Driver laughed.

Then His expression became serious.

"Before you reach the Kingdom…"

The bus grew quiet.

The Driver's voice lowered.

"Each of you will face the thing you fear most."

Abigail sat quietly with that.

She had always believed that if she simply worked hard enough, planned wisely enough, served faithfully enough, she could outrun whatever came next.

She was beginning to understand that self-reliance had never been strength.

It had been a very organized, very capable, very exhausting *form of fear.*

The laughter disappeared.

No one spoke.

No one asked questions.

Because nobody wanted the answer.

Outside, the road curved around the mountain.

And in the distance, barely visible through the sunlight, Hagar noticed something.

A crossroads.

Two roads diverging.

One bright.

One hidden beneath shadow.

A chill moved through her.

For the first time since boarding the bus, she noticed something unsettling.

The Driver's smile had faded.

Rachel looked toward the crossroads.

Then toward Leah.

Without saying a word…

she intertwined her fingers with her sister's.

Leah squeezed gently.

Neither woman knew what waited beyond the mountain.

But neither intended to face it alone.

Ahead…

the crossroads waited.

The bus continued toward the crossroads.

And somewhere deep within every woman, fear and faith began preparing for battle.

CHAPTER EIGHTEEN

The Valley of Decision—A Test of the Heart

The valley appeared without warning.

One moment the bus traveled along the narrow mountain road, fog pressing against the windows like breath against glass. The next moment the mist parted, revealing a vast stone clearing carved into the side of the mountain.

The Driver slowed the bus.

No one spoke.

Ancient pillars circled the clearing. Their surfaces marked with words none of the women could read but somehow understood. The sky above shifted between sunlight and shadow. Clouds moved in unnatural patterns, folding over one another like the heavens were turning pages.

At the center of the clearing stood two roads.

One was bright.

Golden.

Smooth.

Lined with flowers and music.

The other was narrow.

Fog-covered.

Uneven.

Disappearing into darkness.

Rachel leaned forward in her seat.

"Well, that seems obvious."

Her voice carried confidence, but her fingers tightened around the handbag filled with mirrors.

The Driver brought the bus to a complete stop.

The engine grew quiet.

The silence that followed felt alive.

"This is the Valley of Decision," He said.

> *"Multitudes, multitudes in the valley of decision! For the day of the Lord is near in the valley of decision." — Joel 3:14 (NKJV)*

A chill moved through the women.

Hagar clutched her suitcase.

Rebekah rested both hands on her planner.

Leah touched the labels still hanging from her leather bag.

Lot's Wife held her memory box against her chest.

Bathsheba kept one hand over the garment bag at her feet.

Elizabeth stared down at the wooden box of unanswered prayers.

The Woman at the Well held her cracked jar.

Priscilla gathered her heavy shawl around her shoulders.

Mary Magdalene touched the volunteer badges at her shoulder.

Jezebel sat motionless beneath her black armor.

Abigail watched all of them with a counselor's eyes, though her own satchel of burdens weighed heavily beside her.

The Driver opened the bus doors.

"Come."

No one moved at first.

Then Hagar stood.

Elizabeth followed.

One by one, the women stepped off the bus and into the clearing.

The moment their feet touched the stone, the roads changed.

The bright road was no longer one road.

It became many.

Each woman saw something different.

Hagar

Hagar saw a family table.

Her children sat waiting.

Her daughter smiled.

"Mama, come home."

The suitcase in Hagar's hand burst open.

Photographs rose into the air, circling her like birds.

Elizabeth gasped beside her.

Her own bright road had become a nursery.

Yellow walls.

A white crib.

Tiny shoes.

A child's laughter.

The wooden box slipped from her hands and opened at her feet.

Both women stood frozen.

The Driver's voice carried across the clearing.

"The enemy rarely tempts you with what you hate."

Hagar's tears fell freely.

"He tempts you with what you love more than Me."

Hagar took one step forward.

Then another.

No one stopped her.

No one judged her.

Every woman understood what it meant to want something so badly that even an illusion felt like mercy.

Elizabeth reached for her hand.

"I wanted my nursery too," she whispered.

Hagar stopped.

Elizabeth's voice trembled.

"I still do."

The family table flickered.

The nursery shimmered.

The bright road wavered.

Hagar collapsed into Elizabeth's arms.

"I just wanted them to choose me."

Elizabeth held her tightly.

"And I just wanted Him to answer me the way I prayed."

The two women wept together.

One grieving people who left.

One grieving promises that seemed delayed beyond recognition.

Their roads faded.

Not because the longing disappeared.

Because it had been brought into truth.

> *"He heals the brokenhearted and binds up their wounds."* — Psalm 147:3 (NKJV)

Rachel & Leah

Then the clearing shifted.

Rachel's road exploded with applause.

A stage appeared.

Lights.

Crowds.

Cameras.

Women chanting her name.

Her books stacked high.

Her face on screens.

Her beauty admired.

Her influence celebrated.

Her mirrors floated upward, but this time they reflected only her.

Rachel smiled before she could stop herself.

The applause wrapped around her like warmth.

Finally, the mirrors seemed kind.

Leah's road appeared beside hers.

But Leah's was different.

She saw Rachel praised.

Rachel chosen.

Rachel adored.

Again.

The labels on Leah's bag darkened.

Not Chosen.

Leah lowered her eyes.

Rachel took another step toward the bright road.

The applause grew louder.

Her books lined the entrance to the stage.

Women smiled as they spoke her name.

Every mirror floating around her reflected a different version of herself—beautiful, accomplished, admired, confident.

For the first time…

none of them criticized her.

Instead, they whispered,

"You've finally done enough."

"You've finally become enough."

"See? This is what you've been searching for."

Rachel's heart ached.

She hadn't realized how desperately she wanted to hear those words.

The Driver watched quietly.

Rachel turned toward Him.

Tears already filled her eyes.

"What's wrong with wanting this?"

No one answered.

She looked around at the women.

"I'm serious."

Her voice trembled now.

"What's wrong with wanting to believe…"

She struggled to finish the sentence.

"…that I'm finally enough?"

The clearing fell silent.

Even the applause seemed to wait.

Rachel looked back toward the stage.

"I've spent my whole life chasing the next accomplishment…"

"The next compliment…"

"The next opportunity…"

"The next thing that would finally quiet the voice inside me."

She laughed softly through tears.

"But every time I reached it…"

"…there was always another mountain."

She looked back at the Driver.

"I thought if enough people celebrated me…"

"…maybe I'd finally believe what they were saying."

The Driver's expression remained full of compassion.

"It is not wrong to desire joy."

Rachel waited.

"It is not wrong to celebrate the gifts I have placed within you."

He stepped closer.

"But applause can never tell you who you are."

His eyes met hers.

"Because applause is given by people."

"It rises."

"It fades."

"It changes with the crowd."

He paused.

"But your identity was settled long before anyone ever applauded you."

Rachel's tears spilled freely.

The Driver continued.

"You have been searching for enough in the wrong voices."

His gaze softened.

"I settled that question before you ever stepped onto this road."

Rachel lowered her head.

"So why does it feel like You're always asking me to surrender what I want?"

The Driver smiled gently.

"I'm not asking you to surrender joy."

He looked toward the stage.

"I'm asking you to surrender the lie that joy can only be found there."

Rachel followed His gaze.

The applause was still calling her.

The mirrors were still whispering.

"You're finally enough."

Then, somewhere behind her, she heard a familiar voice.

Soft.

Fragile.

"Rachel..."

She froze.

It was Leah.

Not pleading.

Not accusing.

Simply calling her name.

Rachel slowly turned.

She saw her sister standing beneath the weight of the last remaining labels.

For the first time in her life, Rachel understood.

If she walked toward the applause...

she would once again leave Leah standing alone beneath the lie that she had never been chosen.

Rachel looked back toward the stage.

Then back toward her sister.

The applause promised affirmation.

Leah reminded her of love.

Slowly...

painfully...

Rachel stepped away from the stage.

The applause faded.

The mirrors cracked.

And for the first time, Rachel discovered that walking away from the thing she wanted most did not leave her empty.

It led her back to the sister she had almost lost.

Rachel fell to her knees.

"I wanted it," she whispered.

Leah knelt beside her.

"I know."

Rachel looked at her.

"I hated that you had things I didn't."

Leah gave a broken laugh through tears.

"And I hated that people always saw you first."

For the first time, neither woman denied the truth.

Rachel reached toward the darkest label still clinging to Leah's bag.

Not Enough.

Her fingers trembled as she peeled it away.

"This never belonged to you," she whispered.

The label dissolved into light.

Leah looked at her sister through tear-filled eyes.

Then she gently reached toward one of Rachel's cracked mirrors.

Her fingertips rested lightly against the fractured glass.

"Neither did this."

The mirror shimmered.

The cracks disappeared.

Then the entire mirror dissolved into light.

Neither woman spoke.

They didn't need to.

The years of comparison…

the years of misunderstanding…

the years of believing opposite lies…

had finally met in the same place.

Grace.

The Driver watched them for a long moment before speaking.

"The enemy convinced one daughter she was never chosen."

His eyes rested on Leah.

"Then he convinced the other daughter she would never have enough."

He turned toward Rachel.

"One spent her life longing to be chosen."

"The other spent her life trying to become enough."

He smiled gently.

"Neither lie came from Me."

"The enemy has always feared what would happen if you stopped competing with one another… and started carrying one another."

The sisters looked at one another.

For the first time…

They saw what the enemy had always hoped they never would.

They had never competed against each other.

They had been believing different lies from the same enemy.

Rachel reached for Leah's hand.

This time neither of them let go.

Rebekah & Abigail

Across the clearing, Rebekah's road became a hallway of doors.

Behind every door, someone called her name.

"Rebekah!"

"We need you!"

"Fix this!"

"What should we do?"

Her planner flew open.

Pages whipped in the wind.

Abigail moved beside her.

Of all the women, Abigail understood the burden of being needed.

Rebekah tried to laugh.

"They do need me."

Abigail nodded.

"Maybe."

Rebekah looked at her.

"But needing you is not the same as belonging to you."

The words landed hard.

Behind one door, Rebekah saw her son.

Grown.

Moving away.

Building a life beyond her control.

She gripped the planner.

"If I let go, what if everything falls apart?"

The Driver answered:

"Then you will learn I was holding what you never could."

> *"Trust in the Lord with all your heart, and lean not on your own understanding; in all your ways acknowledge Him, and He shall direct your paths."* — Proverbs 3:5–6 (NKJV)

Rebekah stared at the page marked *Daniel.*

Her hands shook.

Abigail placed a steady hand on her back.

"You don't have to tear out the whole planner today."

Rebekah laughed through tears.

"I don't?"

"No," Abigail said.

"Just one page."

Rebekah tore the page slowly.

Painfully.

"He belongs to You," she whispered.

The page turned to light.

Her planner grew lighter.

Abigail's satchel shifted beside her, and one burden inside vanished too.

By helping Rebekah release control, Abigail had released one of her own.

Lot's Wife & Bathsheba

Then Lot's Wife's road appeared.

Her old house stood before her.

Restored.

Beautiful.

The door open.

Her younger self stood on the porch, smiling.

Her business sign shone in the distance.

Her husband waited beside the mailbox.

Everything she had lost was back.

Her memory box opened.

Photographs spilled across the stone.

Lot's Wife walked toward the house.

Bathsheba saw her moving and immediately understood.

Not because she longed for yesterday.

Because she was still imprisoned by it.

"Don't," Bathsheba said.

Lot's Wife shook her head.

"You don't understand."

"I do."

Lot's Wife turned, angry now.

"No, you don't. You're trying to get away from your past. I'm trying to get mine back."

Bathsheba stepped closer.

"And both of us are still letting yesterday name us."

The words stopped her.

The house flickered.

The husband blurred.

The younger self on the porch smiled sadly, then faded.

Lot's Wife covered her mouth as the illusion disappeared.

Bathsheba reached for her hand.

"I know what it is to be trapped behind you."

Lot's Wife wept quietly.

Together they turned away from the house.

> *"Forgetting those things which are behind and reaching forward to those things which are ahead, I press toward the goal for the prize of the upward call of God in Christ Jesus."* — Philippians 3:13–14 (NKJV)

Then Bathsheba's road became a courtroom.

Accusations filled the air.

Failure.

Guilty.

Disqualified.

Unworthy.

Her garment bag opened, and the crown rose beside the old mirror.

The Woman at the Well walked to her side.

"I know that voice," she said.

Bathsheba trembled.

"What if God still sees it?"

The Woman at the Well looked toward the Driver.

Then back at Bathsheba.

"If He came to a well for me, He could come to a courtroom for you."

The mirror cracked.

Bathsheba reached toward the crown.

Her fingers brushed it.

Not ready to wear it.

But ready to believe it belonged near her.

The courtroom faded.

The Woman at the Well & Priscilla

Beside them, the Woman at the Well's road became a line of men, each holding out a cup.

Each promised love.

Each promised belonging.

Each promised to fill the empty place.

Her cracked jar shook in her hands.

Priscilla moved beside her, the heavy shawl slipping from one shoulder.

"You don't have to drink from every cup offered to you."

The Woman at the Well gave a tearful smile.

"And you don't have to disappear to be loved."

Priscilla froze.

The words reached the hidden place beneath her shawl.

Her own road opened.

A perfect home.

A perfect marriage.

A perfect image.

Everyone praised her.

Such a godly wife.

Such a quiet woman.

Such a good example.

But inside the house, her voice was missing.

The shawl tightened around her throat.

Mary Magdalene rushed to her side.

"Breathe."

Priscilla clawed at the fabric.

"I thought silence made me holy."

Mary's eyes filled.

"No. Love makes you holy. Truth makes you free."

> *"And you shall know the truth, and the truth shall make you free."* — John 8:32 (NKJV)

Priscilla pulled one edge of the shawl loose.

The words *Stay Quiet* faded from the fabric.

She inhaled sharply.

The house disappeared.

Mary Magdalene

Mary Magdalene barely had time to steady Priscilla before her own road opened.

A ministry platform stretched before her.

Thousands applauded.

People spoke her name with reverence.

Leader.

Servant.

Faithful one.

The badges at her shoulder glowed.

Every hidden desire to be noticed rose inside her.

Then another image appeared beyond the stage.

Jesus.

Standing alone.

Waiting.

No crowd around Him.

No applause.

Just Him.

The Driver's voice was tender.

"Mary, would you still follow Me if no one ever noticed?"

Mary's face crumpled.

The badges suddenly felt heavy.

The stage called to her.

Jesus did not.

He simply waited.

Mary removed one badge.

Then another.

Her hands shook.

"I want to be seen," she confessed.

The Driver smiled.

"You are."

The stage vanished.

Jesus remained.

Mary wept as Priscilla held her.

Jezebel

Then the atmosphere changed.

The temperature dropped.

Jezebel's road did not become a family, a stage, a courtroom, or a house.

It became a throne room.

Black marble.

Golden walls.

Servants bowing.

Enemies kneeling.

No betrayal.

No weakness.

No need.

No pain.

At the center stood a throne.

Jezebel stared at it.

Every line of her body went still.

The armor gleamed.

The missing piece near her shoulder burned where it had once been whole.

The Driver stepped beside her.

"Sit."

The women looked at Him, startled.

Jezebel narrowed her eyes.

"What?"

"Sit."

Suspicion crossed her face, but temptation was stronger.

She walked to the throne.

Slowly.

Proudly.

As if she had been born for it.

The moment she sat, iron chains erupted from the throne and locked around her wrists.

Jezebel gasped.

The women cried out.

She tried to rise.

She could not.

The throne held her.

The crown above her head became a cage.

The servants vanished.

The gold darkened.

The power she had desired became prison.

The Driver's voice was steady.

"This is what control gives you."

Jezebel pulled against the chains.

Her armor tightened until she winced.

"It keeps you seated where I never called you to stay."

> *"Pride goes before destruction, and a haughty spirit before a fall."* —
> Proverbs 16:18 (NKJV)

Mary Magdalene stepped forward.

Jezebel snapped, "Don't."

Mary stopped.

But she did not leave.

"You don't have to stay there," Mary said.

Jezebel laughed bitterly.

"You think I don't know that?"

But her voice broke.

The missing piece of armor burned brighter.

The exposed place hurt.

It terrified her.

It reminded her of what she could still feel.

With a cry of rage, Jezebel tore one small piece of armor from her forearm and threw it to the ground.

The chains snapped.

The throne cracked.

The room collapsed into fog.

Jezebel stood trembling in the clearing.

Her face was pale.

Her armor was incomplete in two places now.

She covered one exposed opening with her hand.

Mary took one step closer.

This time Jezebel did not tell her to stop.

The Clearing

The clearing fell silent.

Every illusion had faded.

Every woman stood shaken.

No one had passed perfectly.

No one had failed completely.

The Driver looked at them all.

"The bright road showed what you wanted."

His gaze moved toward the place where the shadowed road had been.

"The dark road showed what you feared."

Priscilla whispered, "Which one leads to the Kingdom?"

The Driver's answer was gentle.

"The one where you follow Me."

> *"Your word is a lamp to my feet and a light to my path."* — Psalm 119:105 (NKJV)

The women stood together in the center of the clearing.

Then something beautiful happened.

Without instruction, they moved toward one another.

Hagar reached for Elizabeth.

Rachel reached for Leah.

Rebekah and Abigail stood shoulder to shoulder.

Bathsheba took Lot's Wife by the hand.

The Woman at the Well slipped her arm through Priscilla's.

Mary Magdalene stood beside Jezebel.

Jezebel did not lean into her.

But she did not step away.

For a moment, the women formed a circle.

No one prayed aloud.

No one preached.

No one tried to explain what had happened.

They simply stood together, wounded and honest, breathing the same mountain air.

The Driver watched them with quiet joy.

Then He said:

"Now you are beginning to understand the road."

One by one, the women climbed back onto the bus.

Not one returned the same way she had stepped off.

The doors closed.

The engine rumbled to life.

The bus pulled away from the clearing.

For several minutes no one spoke.

They watched the crossroads through the rear windows.

The bright road remained.

The dark road remained.

Then Leah frowned.

"Wait."

Everyone turned.

"What?" Rachel asked.

"The roads."

They all looked back.

The bright road began to fade.

The family tables disappeared.

The nursery dissolved.

The stage vanished.

The old house crumbled into mist.

The courtroom collapsed.

The cups vanished.

The perfect home disappeared.

The ministry platform faded.

The throne room evaporated.

Then the dark road vanished too.

The fog lifted.

The rocks disappeared.

The shadows withdrew.

Within moments, both roads were gone.

Only one ordinary road remained, winding through the mountains.

Bathsheba whispered, "They weren't real."

The Driver looked at them through the mirror.

"The roads were never the test."

Silence filled the bus.

"The crossroads only revealed what already lived inside you."

Rachel looked down at her broken mirrors.

Hagar touched her suitcase.

Elizabeth held her wooden box.

Rebekah rested her hand on the torn place in her planner.

Lot's Wife closed her memory box.

Bathsheba touched the crown.

The Woman at the Well held her cracked jar.

Priscilla loosened her shawl.

Mary Magdalene touched the empty space where her badges had been.

Jezebel stared at the missing pieces in her armor.

The Driver's voice softened.

"The greatest battles are never fought ahead of you."

Their eyes met in the mirror.

"They are fought within you."

> *"For though we walk in the flesh, we do not war according to the flesh. For the weapons of our warfare are not carnal but mighty in God for pulling down strongholds."* — 2 Corinthians 10:3–4 (NKJV)

The bus rounded a bend.

The crossroads disappeared.

Ahead, the mountain road narrowed.

The fog returned, thicker than before.

But now something moved inside it.

Images.

Faint at first.

Then clearer.

A desert.

A well.

A tent.

A palace.

A salt-covered plain.

A nursery.

A courtroom.

A tomb.

Each image appeared for only a moment before dissolving back into mist.

The women leaned toward the windows.

Hagar's breath caught.

"I know that place."

Rebekah whispered, "So do I."

The Driver did not look back.

But His voice filled the bus.

"The road has shown you your hearts."

The fog brightened.

"Now it will show you your stories."

No one moved.

No one breathed.

Outside the windows, the past began to awaken.

And the bus drove straight into memory.

CHAPTER NINETEEN

The Revelation

The bus traveled deeper into the fog.

Outside the windows, time no longer seemed to move forward.

It folded.

Bent.

Opened.

The mountains disappeared.

The road vanished.

The women sat surrounded by white mist so thick it looked as though the bus was floating between worlds.

No one spoke.

After the tests at the Valley of Decision, each woman carried a new awareness of herself.

And that awareness was uncomfortable.

Not the kind of discomfort that comes from pain.

The kind that comes from clarity.

From finally seeing yourself without the careful filter you had spent years constructing.

The Driver's voice finally broke the silence.

"The road has shown you your hearts."

The women listened.

"Now it will show you your history."

The fog brightened.

Then the first vision appeared.

Hagar

Burden: Abandonment

The wilderness emerged.

Heat. Dust. Isolation.

A mother and child beneath a burning sky, cast out, forgotten, left to survive what no woman should survive alone.

Hagar recognized her immediately.

The biblical Hagar had not wandered into the wilderness by accident.

She had been sent there.

By the very people who claimed to need her.

The Driver's voice moved through the vision like water.

"She believed abandonment was her identity."

Hagar on the bus lowered her head.

The suitcase sat heavy against her ankles.

She had packed it so carefully. Every piece of evidence that she had been left. Every memory of being the one who was dismissed when she was no longer convenient.

She had carried it so long she had stopped noticing the weight.

"But heaven knew her as seen."

The well appeared.

Water flowed.

Hope returned.

Not because her circumstances changed.

But because God spoke first.

"Then she called the name of the Lord who spoke to her, You-Are-the-God-Who-Sees; for she said, 'Have I also here seen Him who sees me?'"
— Genesis 16:13 (NKJV)

Hagar wept.

Not with grief this time.

With recognition.

Her story was not abandonment.

It was survival.

It was being seen by the One who never once looked away.

Rebekah

Burden: Control

The scene shifted.

A tent. Two sons. A promise.

Then manipulation. Planning. Interference. Fear dressed as faithfulness.

The biblical Rebekah had heard from God directly.

The older shall serve the younger.

She believed it.

But she did not trust it.

So, she moved ahead of it.

The modern Rebekah gripped her planner.

The Driver spoke.

"She trusted God's promise."

The vision changed.

Jacob fled. The family fractured. The plan succeeded and still everything fell apart.

"But she did not trust God's timing."

Rebekah closed her eyes.

The torn page in her planner felt heavier than it had before.

She had believed that helping God meant managing the outcome.

She had confused faith with administration.

She had called it wisdom.

The Driver called it something else.

> *"For My thoughts are not your thoughts, nor are your ways My ways," says the Lord. — Isaiah 55:8 (NKJV)*

Rebekah did not open her planner.

But she stopped holding it quite so tightly.

Leah

Burden: I Was Never Chosen

The wedding appeared.

The deception. The morning light. The moment Jacob realized who he had married, and the way his face changed when he did.

Leah watched herself in the vision.

Not with anger.

With grief.

Because she remembered that morning. Not the biblical morning, *her* morning. The one she had replayed in a hundred different forms across her entire life.

The moment when someone looked at her and chose someone else.

She had spent years trying to earn what had already been decided before she could speak.

Naming sons after unmet needs.

Maybe now he'll love me.

Maybe now he'll choose me.

Maybe now I'll be enough.

The labels seemed to tighten.

Overlooked. Plain. Second choice.

The Driver spoke gently.

"Leah spent years trying to earn what God had already given."

The vision shifted.

Judah was born.

And something in Leah changed.

Not because Jacob finally looked at her differently.

But because she stopped waiting for him too.

She began to cry.

Because she finally saw it.

Her identity was never supposed to come from Jacob.

It had always come from somewhere far older than love.

And the lineage that would carry the Savior of the world ran through her.

The one who was never chosen.

> *"And she conceived again and bore a son, and said, 'Now I will praise the Lord.' Therefore, she called his name Judah."* — Genesis 29:35 (NKJV)

Leah pressed her hand to the labels.

She did not remove them yet.

But for the first time, she questioned whether they had ever been true.

Rachel

Burden: I Never Have Enough

The vision shifted, and Leah recognized her immediately.

Of course she did.

She was her sister.

Beauty. Favor. Admiration. Love.

Rachel had everything that the world said mattered.

And still dissatisfaction.

Still longing for the one thing she did not have.

Leah watched the biblical Rachel reach desperately for what Leah possessed.

And Leah felt something unexpected move through her.

Not jealousy.

Grief.

Because she saw it now. What she had not been able to see from inside her own wound.

Rachel had been suffering too.

Just differently.

The mirrors in Rachel's hands caught the light.

The Driver's voice softened.

"She had what everyone wanted."

The vision darkened.

"But she could not enjoy what she already had."

Rachel looked away.

The truth landed quietly.

Not like an accusation.

Like a diagnosis.

She looked at Leah across the aisle.

Leah was already looking at her.

Neither of them spoke.

But something passed between them. The wordless acknowledgment of two women who had spent their whole lives measuring themselves against each other, only to discover they had been reaching for the same thing all along.

To be enough.

To be seen.

To be full.

> *"Now godliness with contentment is great gain."* — 1 Timothy 6:6 (NKJV)

Rachel looked back at her mirrors.

She had spent so long looking at her reflection.

She was only beginning to learn how to look through it.

Lot's Wife

Burden: Yesterday

The city burned.

Angels led the family forward.

The command was simple.

Do not look back.

Lot's Wife had not moved from her seat since the Valley of Decision.

While the other women wept and reached and questioned, she had simply sat. Hands folded, eyes distant, turned toward something no one else on the bus could see.

The Driver's eyes found her through the mirror.

"Lot's Wife carried yesterday."

She said nothing.

But her hands tightened slowly around the memory box in her lap.

The vision showed the biblical woman turn.

One glance.

One longing.

One refusal to release what was already gone.

Salt.

Stillness.

Silence.

The Driver spoke.

"The danger was not memory."

Lot's Wife looked up.

"The danger was worshiping what was behind her."

The memory box trembled in her lap.

> *"Remember Lot's wife."* — Luke 17:32 (NKJV)

Three words.

A warning preserved across centuries.

She pressed her hand against the lid.

She understood now why the Driver had brought her here.

She had been turning back long before she ever boarded the bus.

The road behind them had already curved out of sight.

There was nothing back there to return to.

She knew that.

She just hadn't stopped looking.

Bathsheba

Burden: Shame

A palace emerged.

Loss. Grief. Scandal. Consequences that arrived before she ever had a choice.

The vision refused to simplify her story.

It refused to make her only a victim.

And it refused to make her only a symbol.

It showed her as she was.

A woman whose life had been interrupted by power she did not invite.

The crown sat in Bathsheba's hands.

She had been holding it since she boarded.

Still not wearing it.

Then something shifted in the vision.

The biblical Bathsheba grew older.

Stronger.

Wiser.

A queen mother.

A voice in the throne room.

A name written into the lineage of redemption.

The Driver smiled.

"Her story did not end where people stopped telling it."

Bathsheba touched the crown.

Perhaps hers wouldn't either.

> *"For all have sinned and fall short of the glory of God, being justified freely by His grace through the redemption that is in Christ Jesus." — Romans 3:23–24 (NKJV)*

The same woman.

Two different moments.

One defined by what was done to her.

One defined by who she became after.

Bathsheba held the crown with both hands.

Still not wearing it.

But no longer afraid to hold it.

Priscilla (*The Submissive Wife)*

Burden: Silence

A home church appeared.

Teaching. Leadership. Wisdom. Partnership.

The biblical Priscilla stood beside her husband.

Not behind him.

Beside him.

Teaching. Correcting. Building.

Her voice was not a disruption.

It was a ministry.

The Driver looked directly at modern Priscilla.

"God never required silence to prove submission."

The shawl around her shoulders loosened.

> *"Greet Priscilla and Aquila, my fellow workers in Christ Jesus."* — Romans 16:3 (NKJV)

Fellow workers.

Not followers.

Not background figures.

Partners.

Priscilla stared at the vision.

For the first time, she saw herself clearly.

Not as a woman who had been silenced.

But as a woman who had silenced herself.

The difference mattered.

Because one could be undone by someone else.

The other could only be undone by her.

She reached up slowly.

And loosened the shawl one more time.

The Woman at the Well

Burden: False Love

The well appeared.

Noon sun. Isolation. The particular shame of being seen by no one and everyone at once.

Then Jesus.

Not avoiding her.

Seeking her.

The Woman at the Well looked at the cracked jar in her hands.

The vision showed the biblical woman arriving thirsty.

Not just for water.

For something she had been trying to fill with every relationship, every promise, every man who had offered belonging and delivered something far less.

She had spent her life offering pieces of herself in exchange for love.

She was still learning that love was never supposed to cost her that.

The Driver's voice was quiet.

"She came thirsty."

The woman on the bus whispered:

"And left satisfied."

> *"The woman then left her waterpot, went her way into the city, and said to the men, 'Come, see a Man who told me all things that I ever did.'"*
> —John 4:28–29 (NKJV)

She left her jar behind.

The Woman at the Well looked at the cracked jar in her hands.

The only One who had ever offered her water without a price had been sitting across from her at a well she almost didn't stop at.

Not yet.

She turned the jar slowly in her hands.

But soon.

Mary Magdalene

Burden: Performance

The vision appeared.

The garden. The tomb. The tears.

Then a voice.

"Mary."

The risen Christ called her by name.

Not by her past.

Not by her usefulness.

Not by what she had done or failed to do.

By her name.

The Driver spoke softly.

"She was seen before she was useful."

The words healed something deep inside her.

> *"Jesus said to her, 'Mary!' She turned and said to Him, 'Rabboni!' (which is to say, Teacher)."* — John 20:16 (NKJV)

He said her name.

Just her name.

And it was enough.

Mary pressed her hand to her chest.

She had spent years believing she had to earn the right to be called.

He had called her name before she ever picked up a single badge.

She looked down at the collection of badges in her lap.

Servant. Helper. Available. Reliable.

She had worn them like armor.

She was beginning to understand they were something else entirely.

Jezebel

Burden: Armor

The palace darkened.

Power. Control. Manipulation.

Fear dressed as strength.

The biblical Jezebel ruled.

But she trusted no one.

Loved no one.

Surrendered nothing.

The palace became a prison.

The throne became a cage.

The crown became the loneliest place in the kingdom.

Jezebel stared at the vision.

The missing pieces of armor burned where they had been removed.

The exposed places felt unbearable.

For the first time, she saw her future if she never changed.

And it terrified her.

> *"Pride goes before destruction, and a haughty spirit before a fall."* — Proverbs 16:18 (NKJV)

She had announced herself by her armor.

By her title.

By her reputation.

But the Driver looked at the missing pieces.

At the exposed places.

At what was underneath.

And He did not flinch.

Jezebel's jaw tightened.

She looked away from the vision.

But the image stayed.

The throne that became a prison.

The power that left her utterly alone.

She had called it strength for so long.

She was only now beginning to name it correctly.

Fear.

Elizabeth

Burden: Certainty

The vision became a home.

Years of waiting.

Years of silence.

Years of prayers that seemed to dissolve before they reached the ceiling.

Years of watching others receive what she had asked for and been denied.

Elizabeth sat with her hands folded.

Still.

Composed.

The way she had learned to be when she didn't know what else to do.

Then suddenly—Promise fulfilled.

John.

Joy.

Wonder.

A miracle that arrived long after she had stopped expecting it.

Yet the Driver added quietly:

"Not every faithful prayer receives the answer it expects."

Elizabeth's eyes filled.

The statement landed gently.

But it was true.

And somehow truth felt kinder than false comfort.

She had spent years measuring her faithfulness by the answer.

> *"But those who wait on the Lord shall renew their strength; they shall mount up with wings like eagles, they shall run and not be weary, they shall walk and not faint."* — Isaiah 40:31 (NKJV)

Elizabeth exhaled slowly.

The Driver was not asking her to stop believing.

He was asking her to stop grading her faith by the outcome.

Faithfulness was not a formula.

It was a posture.

And she had held it longer than she knew.

Abigail

Burden: It's All Up To Me

The final vision appeared.

A foolish husband.

An approaching disaster.

A woman standing between destruction and peace, armed with nothing but wisdom, humility, and the willingness to act when everyone else froze.

The biblical Abigail moved quickly.

Not in panic.

In clarity.

She did not wait for permission.

She did not wait for rescue.

She moved.

Modern Abigail sat perfectly still.

The Driver smiled.

"She could not control everyone."

The vision showed Abigail kneeling.

Listening.

Trusting something larger than her own plan.

"But she knew when to act and when to surrender."

> *"Then Abigail made haste…"* — 1 Samuel 25:18 (NKJV)

Abigail looked toward Rebekah.

The lesson belonged to both of them.

Wisdom and control looked similar from the outside.

But they felt entirely different on the inside.

One moved in peace.

The other moved in fear.

Abigail reached into her satchel.

She had always believed that if she planned wisely enough, served faithfully enough, moved quickly enough, she could outrun whatever came next.

She was beginning to understand that self-reliance had never been strength.

It had been a very organized, very capable, very exhausting form of fear.

She removed one burden from the satchel.

And set it beside her feet.

The Revelation

The visions faded.

The fog returned.

No one spoke.

No one moved.

The silence felt sacred.

Then Rachel whispered:

"So, we're not just learning about them."

The Driver nodded.

"No."

Leah looked at her sister across the aisle.

"We're learning about ourselves."

The Driver smiled.

"Exactly."

The women sat quietly.

Each holding her object.

The suitcase.

The planner.

The labels.

The mirrors.

The memory box.

The crown.

The cracked jar.

The shawl.

The badges.

The broken armor.

The satchel.

Twelve women.

Twelve stories.

Twelve lessons still being learned.

And one Kingdom ahead.

Then something extraordinary happened.

The objects began to glow.

Not brightly.

Gently.

Each object projected a single word onto the floor of the bus.

Seen. Trust. Chosen. Contentment. Forward. Redeemed. Wait. Satisfied. Voice. Beloved. Surrender. Wisdom.

The women stared.

Twelve words illuminated the floor like a mosaic of light.

Twelve lessons.

Twelve invitations.

Each one personal.

Each one precise.

Each one waiting to be received.

The Driver finally spoke.

"These are the lessons the road is trying to teach."

> *"Now all these things happened to them as examples, and they were written for our admonition."* — 1 Corinthians 10:11 (NKJV)

The bus entered deeper fog.

The glow faded slowly.

Ahead, ancient voices seemed to whisper from the mist.

Warnings.

Promises.

Prophecies.

And for the first time since boarding the bus, the women understood:

The biblical stories were not merely history.

They were invitations.

The women looked at one another.

Not as strangers.

Not as rivals.

As witnesses.

Each one had seen the other's story laid bare.

Each one had heard the other's wound named.

Each one had watched the other reach toward something they were not yet sure they deserved.

Rachel looked at Leah.

Leah was already looking back.

They had spent so many years measuring themselves against each other.

And here in the fog, in the glow, in the quiet, they were finally seeing each other clearly.

Not as competition.

As sisters.

Somehow that made the journey feel less impossible.

The Driver's voice came quietly from the front.

"The Valley of Decision showed you what lived inside your hearts."

"The Revelation revealed truths. It uncovered what has been hidden."

The women listened.

"What lies ahead is different."

A pause.

"There, you will be asked to bury it."

No one spoke.

Because they understood.

Being exposed was one thing.

Letting go was another.

Far ahead, unseen by the women, the road narrowed once more.

And waiting beyond the fog was not another test.

It was a grave.

Twelve of them.

One for each woman.

Each one waiting to receive something she had carried far too long.

> *"And we know that all things work together for good to those who love God, to those who are the called according to His purpose."* —
> Romans 8:28 (NKJV)

CHAPTER TWENTY
The Crossroads of Identity

The bus stopped.

No one asked why.

They already knew.

This was not the Valley of Decision.

That crossroads had shown them what lived inside their hearts—desires and fears dressed up as roads, tempting them with what they loved and terrifying them with what they feared.

This place was different.

The Valley of Decision had been a test.

This was about identity.

This was about becoming.

Ever since leaving that mountain clearing, something had been shifting inside each of them.

The tests had exposed them.

The visions had explained them.

Now the road had brought them here.

The place where explanation ended.

And choice began.

Outside the windows, the fog parted slowly.

Not revealing a destination.

Revealing a cemetery.

At least that was what it felt like.

A mountain clearing stretched beneath a silver sky.

Twelve stone markers stood in a circle.

Twelve names.

Twelve choices.

Twelve graves waiting to be filled.

The Driver stood.

For a long moment, He said nothing.

The women rose from their seats and followed Him into the cold mountain air.

The wind carried no birdsong.

No music.

Only stillness.

Holy stillness.

The kind that exists inside a sanctuary.

Or beside a grave.

Rachel immediately felt it.

"Why does this place feel sad?"

The Driver looked at her.

"Because something is about to die."

Silence fell over the mountain.

No one laughed.

No one questioned Him.

Because every woman already knew.

The thing dying was not a person.

It was a version of herself.

And somehow that felt just as frightening.

> *"I have been crucified with Christ; it is no longer I who live, but Christ lives in me."* — Galatians 2:20 (NKJV)

The Driver stepped into the center of the circle.

"You have spent years carrying identities that helped you survive."

The women listened.

"They protected you."

A pause.

"They explained your pain."

Another pause.

"They gave meaning to your wounds."

The Driver's eyes moved from woman to woman.

"But they can no longer travel where you are going."

A chill moved through the group.

The stone markers began glowing.

Each one revealed two things.

One identity.

One invitation.

And the mountain trembled.

The funerals began.

Hagar

Burden: Abandonment

She saw the word.

ABANDONED

The sight struck her harder than she expected.

Because she realized something she had never allowed herself to name.

Abandoned had been more than a wound.

It had become a companion.

A terrible companion.

But a familiar one.

The identity had protected her from disappointment.

If nobody stays…

then nobody can hurt you.

Tears filled her eyes.

The suitcase sat beside her feet.

She had packed it so carefully. Every piece of evidence that she had been left, every memory of being dismissed when she was no longer convenient.

She had carried it so long she had stopped noticing the weight.

The Driver spoke softly.

"You learned how to survive being left."

Hagar nodded.

"But now you must learn how to live while being loved."

The words shattered her.

Elizabeth immediately moved beside her.

Not speaking.

Simply standing.

Because she understood grief.

Together they watched the word *Abandoned* dissolve into dust.

Hagar cried as though burying a friend.

Because she was.

> *"Fear not, for I have redeemed you; I have called you by your name; you are Mine." — Isaiah 43:1 (NKJV)*

Rebekah

Burden: Control

Pages erupted from her planner.

Years of plans.

Years of fixing.

Years of carrying responsibilities nobody asked her to carry.

The Driver revealed something she had never considered.

Control had once protected a frightened little girl.

A little girl who learned early that adults could not always be trusted.

That if she didn't hold everything together, everything would fall apart.

So, she held.

And held.

And held.

Until holding became the only thing she knew how to do.

Rebekah began crying before she understood why.

Because suddenly she saw it clearly.

She wasn't burying control.

She was burying the little girl who thought everything depended on her.

Abigail wrapped an arm around her shoulders.

Neither woman spoke.

Both understood what it meant to carry what was never meant to be carried alone.

Together they mourned.

> *"Cast your burden on the Lord, and He shall sustain you; He shall never permit the righteous to be moved."* — Psalm 55:22 (NKJV)

Leah

Burden: I Was Never Chosen

The labels returned.

Not Chosen.

Second Best.

Unwanted.

The words hung around her neck like chains she had grown so accustomed to wearing she had forgotten they were chains at all.

Leah stared at them.

Then looked across the circle at Rachel.

Her sister.

Rachel looked back.

And for the first time, truly for the first time, Rachel saw what those labels had cost her.

Not a rival.

Her sister.

Years.

Decades.

A lifetime of walking into every room already convinced she was the wrong choice.

Rachel stepped forward.

Without speaking.

Without apologizing.

She simply reached up and removed the first label.

Then the second.

Then the third.

Both women cried.

Because rejection was dying.

And even painful identities leave empty spaces behind.

The space where a wound used to live can feel like loss before it feels like freedom.

> *"The Lord has appeared of old to me, saying: 'Yes, I have loved you with an everlasting love; therefore with lovingkindness I have drawn you.'"* — Jeremiah 31:3 (NKJV)

Rachel

Burden: I Never Have Enough

The mirrors appeared.

Thousands of reflections.

Thousands of measurements.

Thousands of reasons she had never felt enough.

Rachel reached toward them.

Then stopped.

The Driver asked quietly:

"What are you afraid will happen if comparison dies?"

The question stunned her.

Because she knew the answer immediately.

"I won't know who I am."

Silence fell over the mountain.

Then Leah took her hand.

Her sister.

"You'll finally find out."

Rachel collapsed into tears.

The mirrors shattered.

Not violently.

Beautifully.

Like glass turning into stars.

She had spent her whole life measuring herself against Leah. Against everyone. And she had never once stopped to ask what she actually wanted.

Who she actually was.

Apart from the comparison.

Apart from the competition.

Apart from the mirror.

> *"For we dare not class ourselves or compare ourselves with those who commend themselves. But they, measuring themselves by themselves, and comparing themselves among themselves, are not wise."* — 2 Corinthians 10:12 (NKJV)

Lot's Wife

Burden: Yesterday

The memory box shook in her hands.

She had carried it across every mile.

Through every vision.

Through every test.

Through every moment when the road offered her a reason to release it.

And still she had not let it go.

The Driver knelt beside her.

"You are not your past."

Lot's Wife looked at the box.

"But it is all I know."

The Driver placed His hand over hers.

"Then let Me show you what you do not yet know."

She opened the box one final time.

The photographs rose into the air.

The old house.

The old life.

The old self she had been before everything changed.

She watched them float upward.

And she did not reach for them.

She had been turning back long before she ever boarded the bus.

Every morning, she woke up and chose yesterday over today.

Every decision had been made in the shadow of what used to be.

Now she watched it rise.

And let it go.

> *"Do not remember the former things, nor consider the things of old. Behold, I will do a new thing." — Isaiah 43:18–19 (NKJV)*

The photographs dissolved.

The box emptied.

Lot's Wife stood with nothing in her hands.

And somehow felt fuller than she had in years.

Bathsheba

Burden: Shame

The old mirror rose.

The accusations returned.

Failure.

Guilty.

Unworthy.

Bathsheba stood before them.

The Woman at the Well stepped beside her.

"I know that voice," she said quietly.

Bathsheba trembled.

"What if He still sees it?"

The Driver spoke.

"He sees you."

A pause.

"Not it."

Bathsheba looked at the crown beside the mirror.

The crown she had been holding since she boarded.

Still not wearing it.

Still not sure she deserved to.

The Driver nodded.

Slowly, Bathsheba turned the mirror face down.

And picked up the crown.

She did not wear it.

But she held it with both hands now.

And that was enough for now.

> *"As far as the east is from the west, so far has He removed our transgressions from us." — Psalm 103:12 (NKJV)*

Elizabeth

Burden: Certainty

The wooden box of unanswered prayers opened.

Every folded prayer she had ever written rose into the air.

Some had been answered.

Many had not.

At least not the way she had asked.

At least not in the time she had expected.

At least not in the form she had imagined.

Elizabeth looked at the Driver.

"I thought faith meant knowing the outcome."

The Driver looked at her with deep tenderness.

"Faith means trusting Me with the outcome."

Elizabeth exhaled.

The difference was everything.

She had spent years grading her faithfulness by the answer.

Measuring her belief by the result.

Wondering what she had done wrong every time the silence stretched long.

She released the prayers one by one.

Not in despair.

In trust.

"Not my certainty," she whispered.

"Your faithfulness."

> *"Now faith is the substance of things hoped for, the evidence of things not seen."* — Hebrews 11:1 (NKJV)

The Woman at the Well

Burden: False Love

The line of men appeared again.

Each one holding out a cup.

Each one promising to fill what only God could fill.

The cracked jar trembled in her hands.

She had carried it since she boarded.

She had carried it long before that.

The Woman at the Well looked at each cup.

Then looked at the Driver.

"None of them were the answer."

The Driver shook His head.

"No."

"But I kept drinking anyway."

"Yes."

She looked down.

"Why?"

The Driver's voice was gentle.

"Because you did not yet know that you were already full."

She set the cracked jar on the ground.

And did not pick it up again.

She had spent years offering pieces of herself in exchange for belonging.

She was only just beginning to understand that belonging was never supposed to cost her that.

> *"But whoever drinks of the water that I shall give him will never thirst again."* — John 4:14 (NKJV)

Priscilla (*The Submissive Wife)*

Burden: Silence

The shawl wrapped tighter for one final moment.

As if it knew it was dying.

Stay quiet.

Don't be too much.

Disappear and be loved.

Priscilla looked at the Driver.

"I thought my voice was dangerous."

The Driver looked at her steadily.

"Your voice was always meant to be used."

She reached for the shawl.

And pulled.

The fabric tore.

The words dissolved.

Priscilla stood without it for the first time.

Her shoulders straightened.

Her chin lifted.

She looked like someone who had just remembered her own name.

She had not been silenced by the world alone.

She had learned to silence herself.

And that was the burial that mattered most.

> *"For God has not given us a spirit of fear, but of power and of love and of a sound mind."* — 2 Timothy 1:7 (NKJV)

Mary Magdalene

Burden: Performance

The badges returned.

Every one of them.

Faithful.

Servant.

Leader.

Volunteer.

Available.

Always available.

Mary looked at them.

Then looked beyond them.

To the image she had seen at the Valley of Decision. Jesus standing alone.

Waiting.

Not surrounded by applause.

Not counting her contributions.

Just waiting.

"I served because I was afraid You would leave if I stopped."

The Driver looked at her.

"I was there before you ever served."

Mary's hands shook.

She removed the badges one by one.

Each one fell like a small surrender.

Each one hit the ground like a confession she had been holding for years.

She had believed her value lived inside her usefulness.

He had called her name before she ever picked up a single badge.

> *"But God demonstrates His own love toward us, in that while we were still sinners, Christ died for us."* — Romans 5:8 (NKJV)

Abigail

Burden: It's All Up To Me

The worn leather satchel appeared at her feet.

She recognized it instantly.

Its straps were stretched from years of carrying far more than they were ever meant to hold.

She had carried it since she boarded the bus.

She had carried it long before that.

Inside were lists.

Plans.

Solutions.

Responsibilities that belonged to other people.

Promises she had made to herself.

If I don't carry this...

...everything falls apart.

Abigail reached for the satchel.

The Driver gently placed His hand over hers.

"You don't have to pick it up again."

She looked at Him.

"But who will carry it?"

"I will."

Her fingers slowly released the worn leather strap.

For the first time, the satchel remained on the ground.

She had spent years believing that faith meant carrying more.

She was only just beginning to understand that faith sometimes meant laying it down.

"Cast your burden on the Lord, and He shall sustain you." — Psalm 55:22 (NKJV)

Jezebel

Burden: Armor

The mountain grew silent.

Even the wind stopped.

Her stone marker glowed.

ARMOR

The word seemed alive.

The other women watched.

Because everyone knew.

This one was different.

Jezebel stared at the armor covering her body.

The armor had survived betrayal.

The armor had survived abandonment.

The armor had survived humiliation.

The armor had survived heartbreak.

The armor had kept her standing when everything else tried to knock her down.

The Driver stepped forward.

"Tell them."

Jezebel's eyes widened.

"No."

The Driver waited.

The women waited.

The mountain waited.

Finally, her voice broke.

"The last time I trusted someone…"

Silence.

"…they destroyed me."

No one spoke.

No one judged.

Because suddenly every woman understood.

The armor was not pride.

The armor was *pain.*

Mary Magdalene quietly stepped beside her.

Not rescuing.

Not fixing.

Simply staying.

Because she knew what it was to hide behind something that looked like strength.

Tears streamed down Jezebel's face.

"I don't know who I am without it."

The Driver smiled gently.

"Neither do they."

The women looked around the circle.

Because it was true.

None of them knew who they would be without the identities they were burying.

That was what made faith necessary.

> *"There is no fear in love; but perfect love casts out fear, because fear involves torment. But he who fears has not been made perfect in love."* — 1 John 4:18 (NKJV)

Slowly.

Painfully.

Jezebel removed another piece of armor.

Then another.

Each piece hit the ground like a funeral bell.

The mountain echoed.

And for the first time in years, Jezebel looked small.

Human.

Free.

The Birthplace

When it was over, the women stood together in exhausted silence.

Around them lay the remains of old identities.

A battered suitcase, emptied.

Torn planner pages.

Dissolved labels.

Shattered mirrors turned to stars.

Faded photographs rising skyward.

A cracked jar set gently on the ground.

A torn shawl.

Scattered badges.

A weathered leather satchel.

Broken armor.

A memory box, empty and still.

A wooden box of released prayers.

Twelve women.

Twelve burdens laid down.

Twelve graves filled.

The Driver pointed toward the ground.

"Look."

The women did.

Rachel whispered first.

"All I see is loss."

The Driver nodded.

"Look again."

Silence.

Then Hagar noticed something.

Elizabeth stood taller.

Bathsheba looked lighter.

Priscilla looked stronger.

Mary seemed peaceful.

Even Jezebel was breathing differently.

The Driver asked:

"What else do you see?"

This time Abigail answered.

Her voice trembled.

"Freedom."

The Driver smiled.

"Yes."

And suddenly every woman understood.

The mountain was not a cemetery.

It was a birthplace.

The old identities had died.

But something new was beginning to live.

> *"Therefore, if anyone is in Christ, he is a new creation; old things have passed away; behold, all things have become new." — 2 Corinthians 5:17 (NKJV)*

The Gate

Ahead, the gateway opened.

Golden light spilled across the mountain.

Music drifted from beyond.

Warmth touched their faces.

Hope rose inside them.

The women smiled through tears.

Then they looked beyond the gate.

And their smiles faded.

Another road waited.

Longer.

Steeper.

Harder.

Rachel groaned.

The others laughed.

Even the Driver smiled.

Then His expression became serious.

"At the Crossroads, you chose who you want to become."

Silence settled over the mountain.

The women listened carefully.

"The road ahead will reveal who you truly are."

No one spoke.

Because they understood.

Choosing freedom was one thing.

Living free was another.

> *"Stand fast therefore in the liberty by which Christ has made us free, and do not be entangled again with a yoke of bondage."* — Galatians 5:1 (NKJV)

The Sisters

The women boarded the bus together.

Not as strangers.

Not as rivals.

Not even as fellow travelers.

As sisters.

Rachel and Leah were the last to board.

They stood for a moment at the door. Two women who had spent their whole lives measuring themselves against each other, standing side by side at the threshold of something neither of them had words for.

Rachel looked at her sister.

"I'm sorry," she said quietly. "For all of it."

Leah shook her head.

"We were both lost."

A pause.

"We just got lost differently."

They boarded together.

And sat beside each other.

For the first time in the entire journey.

The bus rolled forward.

No one spoke.

No one needed to.

The First Glimpse

The mountain cemetery disappeared behind them.

The graves were gone.

The old identities were gone.

Ahead, the fog slowly began to glow.

At first, it looked like moonlight.

Then sunlight.

Then something brighter.

Something *alive.*

The women moved toward the windows.

Hagar was first to see it.

"Driver…"

Her voice trembled.

The others looked up.

Through the fog, far in the distance, twelve pillars of light rose into the sky.

Not mountains.

Not clouds.

Gates.

No one breathed.

Bathsheba clutched her crown.

Elizabeth pressed a trembling hand against her mouth.

Rachel leaned forward in disbelief.

Leah reached over and took her sister's hand.

Even Jezebel forgot to hide her wonder.

The Driver smiled but kept His eyes on the road.

"We're not there yet."

The women stared at the distant light.

Yet none of them looked away.

Because for the first time since boarding the bus, they could see the Kingdom.

And it was closer than they had ever imagined.

> *"Eye has not seen, nor ear heard, nor have entered into the heart of man the things which God has prepared for those who love Him." — 1 Corinthians 2:9 (NKJV)*

CHAPTER TWENTY-ONE
The Kingdom—Gates Open

No one spoke when the light appeared.

It did not arrive the way sunrise arrives, gradually, apologetically, as though unsure of its welcome. It came the way truth comes to a woman who has finally stopped running from it. Certain. Steady. Filling every corner of the sky until there was no shadow left to hide in.

The bus slowed. Not because the road ended. Because something ahead made speed feel irrelevant.

Through the windows, the city emerged. Not all at once, but in layers, the way a woman reveals herself when she finally trusts the room she is standing in. First the light. Then the outline of towers. Then gardens climbing walls that had no business holding gardens. Then streets that seemed to be paved not with gold but with *intention.* As though every stone had been placed with someone specific in mind.

Someone like them.

Hagar pressed her palm flat against the glass.

She had spent her life looking through windows. Watching from the outside. Pressing her face against the glass of other people's belongings and telling herself that the cold on her cheek was just the weather.

This was different.

This glass was warm.

She pulled her hand back and looked at her palm as though it had told her something.

"You are not outside anymore," she said to no one.

But the woman beside her—Abigail—heard it. And nodded. And did not say a word, because some confirmations do not need language.

The gates came into view slowly.

They were not what any of them had imagined. There were no guards. No checkpoints. No long line of women waiting to be evaluated, assessed, found sufficient or found lacking.

There were simply gates.

Tall. Open. Radiating something that was not quite sound and not quite silence but existed in the space between the two. The space where a held breath lives just before it releases.

And then one of them heard it.

Elizabeth.

She had spent decades learning to wait in silence. She knew how to listen for things that had not yet arrived. She had trained her ears on disappointment so long that she had almost forgotten they were built for something else entirely.

She tilted her head.

"Do you hear that?" she whispered.

No one answered immediately. They were all leaning toward the windows now, twelve women pressing gently into the glass, and one by one, they heard it.

The gates were singing.

It was not a hymn anyone recognized. It was not a melody that could be transcribed or taught. It was the kind of sound that bypasses the ear entirely and arrives somewhere deeper. The place in a woman where she stores everything she was never allowed to say out loud.

For Hagar, the singing carried the sound of a name being spoken in the desert. *Her* name. The first time anyone had seen her and called her by what she actually was.

For Leah, it carried something she had never heard directed at her. Not once in all her years of trying. It sounded like: *enough. You were always enough.*

For Rachel, it carried the silence of a woman who had finally stopped counting what she did not have. Not because she had received everything she wanted. But because she had discovered, somewhere on the road between the Valley and this moment, that she had never been empty to begin with.

For Bathsheba, the singing carried a crown being placed. Not taken, not assigned, not used as a tool of someone else's ambition. *Given.* Freely. To her. For her.

She reached up and touched her head without thinking.

For the Woman at the Well, it carried the sound of a conversation that had never ended. A voice that had known her name before she introduced herself. A well that never ran dry.

She pressed her hand to her chest and exhaled long, slow, complete.

For Lot's Wife, the singing carried something she had not expected.

It carried forward.

Not backward. Not the memory of what she had left. Not the pull of what she had lost. It carried the sound of what lay ahead, a direction she had not known how to face until the road buried the past behind her and left her with only one way to go.

She did not look back.

She did not even feel the impulse.

And the absence of that impulse was the most extraordinary thing she had ever felt in her life.

Priscilla sat very still.

The singing reached her like permission.

She had carried silence for so long that she had begun to mistake it for her nature. As though she had been born without a voice worth hearing. As though the words she swallowed each time she was told to step back, sit down, defer, or diminish—as though those words had simply dissolved.

They had not dissolved. They were here. In this sound. Rising.

She opened her mouth.

Not to speak to anyone. Not to teach or explain or justify. Simply to let the sound move through her the way it was meant to—freely, without apology, without asking anyone's permission first.

The woman beside her, Mary Magdalene, heard it and smiled.

Mary Magdalene had been watching Jezebel for the last several minutes.

Jezebel sat apart from the others—not in hostility, but in the old habit of a woman who had learned that the center of any room was a battlefield and the edges were safer. She held herself with the posture of armor. Chin up. Shoulders back. Eyes forward. The stance of a woman who had never once let anyone see her flinch.

The singing reached her differently than it reached the others.

It did not comfort her immediately. It *questioned* her. It moved through the armor and found the woman underneath—the one who had built the armor in the first place, the one who had decided so long ago that softness was a wound waiting to happen.

Jezebel's jaw tightened.

Mary watched her.

She did not intervene. She did not offer comfort. She simply sat close enough that Jezebel would know she was not alone in whatever was happening.

After a long moment, something in Jezebel's posture shifted. Not collapsed. She was not a woman who collapsed. But *released.* The way a fist releases when the thing it has been gripping is finally, finally set down.

She turned to Mary.

"I don't know how to do this," Jezebel said. And her voice was quiet in a way it had never been quiet before. Not silenced. Not suppressed. *Quiet.* The way a woman is quiet when she is finally speaking from the inside rather than performing for the outside.

Mary held her gaze.

"You already did it," Mary said. "Everything you buried at the crossroads. The armor, the strategy, the control. That was the hard part. This part is just walking through."

Jezebel looked at the gates.

"What if I don't remember who I am without all of it?"

Mary considered this. Then:

"What if that's the last lie you have to bury?"

Jezebel was quiet for a long time.

Then, slowly, the corner of her mouth moved.

Not a performance. Not a calculated smile designed to manage a room.

Something real. Something small. Something that looked like the beginning of a woman meeting herself for the first time.

The Driver rose.

He had not spoken since the crossroads. He had driven steadily, without announcement, without urgency, the way someone drives when they know exactly where they are going and have never once doubted the destination.

He turned to face them.

Twelve women. Twelve stories. Twelve burdens buried. Twelve women who had boarded a bus carrying everything they had been told they were and had arrived here carrying only what they actually were.

He looked at each of them.

Not quickly. Not as a survey. The way a person looks at someone they have known for a very long time and at once sees them clearly, perhaps for the first time.

"We're here," He said.

Simple. Sufficient.

"Welcome home."

The doors opened.

The air that came through was not cold and not warm. It was the temperature of *arrival.* The feeling of a place that had been prepared with you in mind, that had held your name on its walls before you knew you were coming.

No one moved immediately.

This was not hesitation. It was the pause of women who had learned, on this road, that some thresholds deserve to be honored before they are crossed.

Hagar stood first.

It was right that she stood first. She had been the first to be sent away. The first to be told she did not belong. The first to discover, in a desert with no witness but God, that belonging was not something another person could grant or revoke.

She walked to the door of the bus.

She stepped down.

Her foot touched the ground of the Kingdom and she stopped.

Not because she was afraid. Because the ground felt like something she had been walking toward her entire life without knowing it had a name.

She looked down at her feet. Then up at the gates. Then back at the women still on the bus.

"It's real," she said. Her voice broke on the last word—not from grief, but from the particular release of a woman who has hoped for something so long that when it arrives, she does not immediately have the language for it.

"It's real. Come."

They came.

One by one, and then together, the way women move when they have stopped competing for the same narrow door and discovered that the entrance was always wide enough for all of them.

Leah stepped off and felt the ground receive her—not just her weight, but *her.* The full weight of her. The years of being overlooked, the children she had named after longing, the prayers she had sent up from a bed where she was present but not chosen.

All of it received. None of it wasted.

Rachel stepped off beside her.

Not behind her. Not ahead of her. *Beside her.*

Their hands found each other without either of them deciding to reach. The way sisters find each other when the rivalry has finally been buried and what remains is just the original thing. Two women from the same place, carrying the same blood, arriving at the same destination.

Leah looked at her.

"No one is second here," she said.

Rachel shook her head slowly, eyes full.

"No. No one."

They walked through the gates together.

Rebekah walked through and felt the plans fall away.

Not her wisdom—her need to control the outcome. The exhausting architecture of strategy and management and steering that she had built around herself because she had not trusted that the right thing would happen without her intervention.

She took one step inside the gates and understood, with the clarity of a woman who has finally stopped arguing with peace, that she could put it down.

She put it down.

She kept walking. Lighter than she had been in years.

Abigail walked through and felt the weight of everyone else's crisis lift from her shoulders.

She had spent her life being the solution to other people's emergencies. She had been wise, yes, but wisdom deployed from fear looks different from wisdom deployed from freedom. She had been wise because she had to be. Because if she wasn't, everything fell apart. Because she had never once believed that anything would hold without her holding it.

She stepped through the gates and felt something hold her.

Not her wisdom. Not her planning. Not her quick action and good judgment.

Something else. Something that had been holding her all along, even when she was too busy holding everything else to notice.

She stopped walking and simply stood still for a moment, receiving it.

Bathsheba walked through, the last of the twelve.

She had been the last to surrender what she carried. She had stood at the crossroads the longest, turning the crown over in her hands, understanding what it meant to lay it down before she was ready to let it go.

She walked through the gates.

And something happened that no one had planned, and no one could have predicted.

The crown she had laid down at the crossroads, the one that had represented every way her body had been used as currency, her name attached to someone else's story, and her identity defined by what had been done to her instead of who she truly was.

It was here.

Not the same crown, not the symbol of shame she had laid down on the road.

A different crown. Clean. Simple. Given, not taken.

The Driver held it in His hands, as though He had been waiting for this moment all along.

She did not lower her eyes.

She looked at the Driver instead.

He smiled.

Then, with gentle hands, He placed the crown upon her head.

The other women watched.

No one applauded. No one needed to. Some moments are too sacred for applause. They simply witnessed her fully, without agenda. The way women witness each other when they have finally learned that another woman's crown does not diminish their own.

Elizabeth walked through the gates and felt time release her.

Not the years—she did not suddenly become young. But the *waiting,* the long, grinding, faith-testing weight of waiting for something that had not come when she expected it, that had made her question whether she had been forgotten, whether her prayers had been heard, whether her faithfulness had mattered.

She stepped through the gates and felt the answer land in her chest like a stone settling to the bottom of clear water.

It had always mattered.

Every prayer. Every year. Every morning, she had chosen to believe when believing was the harder option.

All of it counted. None of it lost.

She pressed her hand to her heart and stood very still, letting the accounting settle.

The gates remained open.

The women stood inside the Kingdom. Some still, some moving slowly through the light, some standing together in the quiet solidarity of women who have survived the same road.

The Driver stood at the threshold.

He did not come in. Not yet. He stood in the doorway between the road and the Kingdom, facing back the way they had come.

Watching. Waiting. Because there were still others to bring home.

There were other women. Other invitations. Other mornings when a woman would wake up and find a small envelope on her kitchen counter, or her nightstand, or tucked inside the pages of a book she had been meaning to read for years.

Other women who were carrying things they had been carrying so long they had forgotten the weight had a name.

The road was still open.

The gates were still open.

And the Driver's expectation had not changed.

Inside the Kingdom, Hagar looked back at him. Not with longing, not with the pull of the past, but with the clear eyes of a woman who understood now what the journey had been for.

She raised her hand.

He nodded.

And the gates stayed open.

> *"Now to Him who is able to keep you from stumbling, And to present you faultless Before the presence of His glory with exceeding joy, To God our Savior, Who alone is wise, Be glory and majesty, Dominion and power, Both now and forever. Amen.* — Jude 1:24–25 (NKJV)

> *"Therefore, if anyone is in Christ, he is a new creation; old things have passed away; behold, all things have become new."* — 2 Corinthians 5:17 (NKJV)

CHAPTER TWENTY-TWO

The Kingdom—Final Reckoning

The Kingdom was not what the women expected.

It was more.

More alive.

More beautiful.

More real.

The air itself seemed filled with purpose.

Rivers sang as they moved over stone.

Trees shimmered with light that appeared to come from within.

Flowers opened as they passed, releasing fragrances that awakened forgotten memories of joy.

> *"And he showed me a pure river of water of life, clear as crystal, proceeding from the throne of God and of the Lamb."* — Revelation 22:1 (NKJV)

The Driver turned from the open gates.

He had watched the road long enough.

Now He turned toward them, fully, completely, and became what He had always been on this journey:

Not just the one who drove them here.

But the one who would show them what *here* actually meant.

He stood before them.

Behind Him stretched the Kingdom.

Ahead of them stretched truth.

Not lessons.

Not tests.

Truth.

The Driver smiled.

"You spent much of your lives asking questions."

The women listened.

"Why did this happen?"

A pause.

"Where were You?"

Another pause.

"Why didn't You stop it?"

The Driver's eyes softened.

"Today, you will see what was hidden."

> *"For now we see in a mirror, dimly, but then face to face. Now I know in part, but then I shall know just as I also am known."* — 1 Corinthians 13:12 (NKJV)

Silence fell.

Then twelve paths appeared.

Not separate destinations.

Different revelations.

The Driver extended His hand.

"Come."

Hagar & Elizabeth

The Driver led them to a valley filled with wells.

Thousands of wells.

Each one reflected moments from their lives.

Hagar immediately recognized hers.

The empty apartment.

The unanswered phone calls.

The nights she cried herself to sleep.

The years she believed nobody stayed.

Elizabeth saw her own.

The waiting.

The silence.

The prayers that seemed to disappear into heaven unanswered.

They watched together.

Then the water changed.

The memories expanded.

Both women gasped.

The Driver had been present in every scene.

Not visible.

But there.

Hagar saw Him sitting beside her when she thought she had been forgotten.

Elizabeth saw Him standing quietly through seasons of waiting.

Then the wells revealed something else.

Doors that never opened.

Dangers they never encountered.

Heartbreaks they never experienced because unseen protection had intervened.

Hagar fell to her knees.

Elizabeth covered her mouth.

Their stories had not been abandonment and unanswered prayers.

They had been preservation.

The Driver smiled.

"You saw what you lost."

The wells shimmered.

"Today you see what was spared."

> *"The Lord is my shepherd; I shall not want… Yea, though I walk through the valley of the shadow of death, I will fear no evil; for You are with me."* — Psalm 23:1, 4 (NKJV)

Hagar pressed both hands to the ground.

The same ground she had once collapsed on in the wilderness.

But this time she was not alone.

She had never been alone.

Elizabeth knelt beside her.

Two women who had waited and wandered finally understanding that every step had been watched.

Every tear had been counted.

Every prayer had been heard.

> *"You number my wanderings; put my tears into Your bottle; are they not in Your book?"* — Psalm 56:8 (NKJV)

Rebekah & Abigail

The Driver led them into a hall lined with doors.

Thousands of doors.

Each one represented a situation they had tried to manage.

A family crisis.

A church problem.

A relationship.

A child.

A decision.

Rebekah immediately recognized the doors she had tried to force open.

Abigail recognized the burdens she had carried without being asked.

The Driver opened the first door.

Inside was a situation both women remembered worrying about endlessly.

God had resolved it without either of them.

The next door revealed another.

And another.

Years of anxiety.

Years of striving.

Years of carrying responsibilities that were never theirs.

Abigail laughed at first.

Then cried.

Rebekah did both at the same time.

"It wasn't all on us."

The Driver smiled.

"It never was."

> *"Trust in the Lord with all your heart, and lean not on your own understanding; in all your ways acknowledge Him, and He shall direct your paths."* — Proverbs 3:5–6 (NKJV)

Rebekah stared at a door she had spent a decade trying to pry open.

It had opened on its own.

On God's schedule.

In God's way.

Without her interference.

She pressed her palm flat against it.

And finally let it close.

Abigail looked at the last door in the hall.

The one she had carried longest.

The burden nobody had asked her to pick up.

The burden she had never put down.

She looked at the Driver.

He nodded.

She set it down.

And walked away without looking back.

> *"And He said to me, 'My grace is sufficient for you, for My strength is made perfect in weakness.'"* — 2 Corinthians 12:9 (NKJV)

Leah & Rachel (The Sisters)

The Driver led them to a lake.

Its surface reflected their lives.

They had walked through the gates as sisters.

They held hands at the threshold.

But this was something different.

This was not reconciliation.

This was revelation.

At first Leah saw every rejection.

Rachel saw every comparison.

Then the water deepened.

The reflections widened.

Leah saw generations touched by her faithfulness.

Rachel saw lives healed because she refused to quit.

Neither woman had known.

Neither woman had seen.

The Driver touched the water.

The reflection expanded until they saw the lineage of kings.

Then something greater.

The lineage of Christ.

Leah covered her face.

Rachel began weeping.

Years spent competing.

Years spent measuring.

Years spent wishing they were each other.

The Driver spoke softly.

"Heaven never compared you."

"For we are His workmanship, created in Christ Jesus for good works, which God prepared beforehand that we should walk in them." — *Ephesians 2:10 (NKJV)*

Leah looked at the water.

She had named sons after longing.

Reuben: *God has seen my affliction.*

Simeon: *God has heard.*

Levi: *Now my husband will be attached to me.*

Judah: *Now I will praise the Lord.*

The Driver traced the names across the water.

"You called out to Me in every name."

Leah wept.

"And I answered in every generation."

Rachel watched the lineage of Christ trace back through Leah's sons.

Through Judah.

Through the tribe that carried the promise.

She looked at her sister.

Not with jealousy.

Not with grief.

With wonder.

"The Lord has done great things for us, and we are glad." — Psalm 126:3 (NKJV)

Leah looked at Rachel.

Rachel looked at Leah.

No words were needed.

They already knew.

They simply held each other—not for the first time, but for the first time fully understanding why.

Not as rivals.

Not as wounds.

As sisters.

As they were always meant to be.

Lot's Wife & Bathsheba

The Driver led them through a corridor of doors.

Behind every door stood a moment they wished they could change.

Lot's Wife saw every backward glance.

Bathsheba saw every accusation.

Every regret.

Every memory.

The women braced themselves.

Expecting judgment.

Instead, they found redemption.

The Driver opened door after door.

God had continued writing after the pain.

Healing had happened.

People had learned.

Lives had changed.

Beauty had emerged from broken places.

"He heals the brokenhearted and binds up their wounds." — Psalm 147:3 (NKJV)

Bathsheba stood before her own final door.

She did not need to reach for a crown.

She was already wearing it.

She had placed it on her head when she stepped through the gates.

She had not yet understood what it meant.

Now she did.

She opened the door.

Inside was not shame.

Not the story others had written about her.

Not the version of her name that had been passed around like a wound.

It was her name.

Her *actual* name.

Spoken by the One who had known her before any of it happened.

Before the palace.

Before the loss.

Before the grief.

Before every voice that had reduced her to a footnote in someone else's story.

She pressed both hands to her chest.

"That's me," she whispered.

The Driver smiled.

"Yes."

He looked at her fully, completely, without condition.

"That has always been you."

Bathsheba stood tall.

Crown on her head.

Shame behind her.

Not because someone had finally given her permission.

Because she had finally stopped waiting for it.

> *"Strength and honor are her clothing; She shall rejoice in time to come."*
> — Proverbs 31:25 (NKJV)

Lot's Wife stood before her own final door.

The Driver paused before it.

He looked at her.

"This one is yours."

She reached for the handle.

Then stopped.

"What's inside?"

The Driver smiled.

"The future."

She opened the door.

Not a ruined city.

Not a pillar of salt.

A garden.

Alive.

Blooming.

Breathing.

Full of everything she had been afraid she would never have again.

Lot's Wife stepped through the doorway.

And did not look back.

> *"Behold, I will do a new thing, now it shall spring forth; shall you not know it? I will even make a road in the wilderness and rivers in the desert."* — Isaiah 43:19 (NKJV)

The Woman at the Well & Priscilla (The Submissive Wife)

The Driver brought them to the River of Life.

The water flowed endlessly.

The Woman at the Well watched as the river divided into streams.

Each stream touched another life.

Then another.

One testimony.

One conversation.

One moment of honesty at a well on an ordinary afternoon.

The ripple effects reached farther than she could imagine.

> *"And the water that I shall give him will become in him a fountain of water springing up into everlasting life."* — John 4:14 (NKJV)

Priscilla watched words she almost never spoke transform lives.

Teaching.

Encouraging.

Guiding.

Strengthening.

The Driver smiled.

"You measured your lives by what you could see."

The river glowed.

"I measured them by what they became."

The Woman at the Well looked at the cracked jar she still carried.

The Driver held out His hand.

She placed it in His palm.

He did not fix it.

He filled it.

Water poured from the cracked places.

Not in spite of the cracks.

Through them.

> *"But we have this treasure in earthen vessels, that the excellence of the power may be of God and not of us." — 2 Corinthians 4:7 (NKJV)*

The Woman at the Well laughed.

The sound echoed across the river.

Priscilla laughed with her.

Priscilla looked at the shawl in her hands.

The last remnant of silence.

She let it fall into the river.

The current carried it away.

And her voice rose to fill the space where it had been.

Clear.

Unashamed.

Free.

> *"For God has not given us a spirit of fear, but of power and of love and of a sound mind."* — 2 Timothy 1:7 (NKJV)

Mary Magdalene

The Driver led Mary into a garden.

The same garden.

The empty tomb.

The morning everything changed.

Mary smiled.

Then cried.

Then smiled again.

"I remember."

The Driver nodded.

The garden expanded.

Mary saw every life strengthened because she remained faithful.

Every person encouraged because she testified.

Every soul influenced because she stayed when others left.

The Driver looked at her.

"You thought your greatest contribution was what you did."

Mary nodded.

The Driver smiled.

"No."

The garden brightened.

"It was that you stayed."

Mary broke into tears.

Not tears of grief.

Tears of understanding.

The garden filled with voices.

Every person Mary had ever encouraged.

Every woman who had heard her testimony and found courage.

Every life that had been changed because one woman stayed at the tomb when everyone else had gone home.

Mary stood in the center of it all.

Not performing.

Not serving.

Not earning.

Simply present.

Simply loved.

Simply home.

Then the Driver said her name.

The way He had said it that morning in the garden.

The morning she turned and recognized Him through her tears.

The morning the world changed.

"Mary."

She turned.

Just as she had turned then.

And the garden held her.

> *"I have called you by your name; you are Mine."* — Isaiah 43:1 (NKJV)

Jezebel

The Driver led Jezebel to a riverbank.

Armor lay scattered along the shore.

The armor she had removed piece by piece on the road.

The armor she had believed she needed.

The armor that had kept her alive and kept her lonely at the same time.

The river reflected her life.

The real life.

Not the version she told others.

The hurt.

The fear.

The betrayals.

The loneliness.

The desperation hidden beneath strength.

Jezebel lowered her head.

The Driver touched the water.

The reflection changed.

She saw every person who had genuinely loved her.

Every opportunity for healing.

Every invitation she rejected because fear felt safer than vulnerability.

Tears streamed down her face.

Then the Driver revealed something unexpected.

Lives she had protected.

People she had inspired.

Strength she had passed on.

Courage she had given others without knowing it.

Even her mistakes had not stopped God from working.

> *"And we know that all things work together for good to those who love God, to those who are the called according to His purpose."* —
> Romans 8:28 (NKJV)

Jezebel stared at the water.

For the first time in her life, she saw herself completely.

Not villain.

Not warrior.

Not failure.

Not survivor.

Beloved.

The truth shattered her.

And healed her.

At the same time.

She looked at the armor on the shore.

Piece by piece.

Battle by battle.

Wound by wound.

She had built a fortress around a heart that only ever wanted to be held.

The Driver knelt beside the last piece of armor.

He did not pick it up.

He waited.

Jezebel reached down.

Her hands trembled.

She picked it up.

Looked at it one final time.

And placed it in the river.

The current took it.

Slowly.

Gently.

Completely.

Jezebel stood on the riverbank with nothing between herself and the world.

No armor.

No title.

No performance.

No fear.

Just her.

Just Him.

Just this.

> *"The Lord your God in your midst, the Mighty One, will save; He will rejoice over you with gladness, He will quiet you with His love, He will rejoice over you with singing."* — Zephaniah 3:17 (NKJV)

She heard it then.

Faint at first.

Then undeniable.

Singing.

Not from the women.

Not from the Kingdom walls.

From above.

Over her.

For her.

Jezebel wept until she had no more tears.

And then she laughed.

The Gathering

The Driver led the women back together.

Twelve women stood beside the River of Life.

No one spoke.

The revelations were too great.

The truth too beautiful.

The Driver looked at them.

One by one.

Hagar.

Rebekah.

Leah.

Rachel.

Lot's Wife.

Bathsheba.

Elizabeth.

The Woman at the Well.

Priscilla.

Mary Magdalene.

Jezebel.

Abigail.

"You thought the road was about finding the Kingdom."

The women listened.

"It was."

The Driver smiled.

"But the Kingdom was never hiding from you."

The river shimmered.

The gardens brightened.

The Kingdom itself seemed to lean closer.

The Driver's voice softened.

"You were learning to see what had been true all along."

He looked at each of them.

"You thought you were finding your way to Me."

The women were still.

"I was finding My way to you."

He paused.

"In every chapter."

"Every wound."

"Every delay."

"Every name you called yourself in the dark."

"Every morning you got up when you had no reason to."

"Every prayer that felt like it disappeared."

"Every door that closed."

"Every wilderness."

"Every well."

"Every garden."

"Every road."

He looked at all twelve of them at once.

"You were never lost."

"You were always being led."

> *"The Lord has appeared of old to me, saying: 'Yes, I have loved you with an everlasting love; therefore with lovingkindness I have drawn you.'"* — Jeremiah 31:3 (NKJV)

The Welcome

The Driver opened His arms.

The Kingdom brightened around Him.

And twelve women who had spent a lifetime searching, finally understood what home felt like.

"Welcome home."

The words were simple.

But they landed differently now.

Not as an announcement.

As a completion.

Everything the road had been building toward.

Every invitation.

Every dream.

Every burden carried to the bus station.

Every step onto the bus.

Every mile through fog and crossroads and valley.

Every burial of old names.

Every gate.

Every threshold crossed.

It had all been leading here.

To this.

To Him.

To these words.

Welcome home.

Hagar wept.

She had been found.

Not just today.

She had been found in the wilderness.

She had been found in the dark.

She had been found every night she cried alone.

She had always been found.

Rebekah exhaled.

A breath she had been holding for decades.

She could finally rest.

The plans were not hers to carry.

They never had been.

Leah lifted her face.

The face that had spent a lifetime turned away.

She had always been chosen.

Not second.

Not overlooked.

Chosen.

From the beginning.

Rachel laughed through tears.

She had always been enough.

Not almost enough.

Not enough if she tried harder.

Enough.

Simply.

Completely.

Enough.

Lot's Wife turned forward.

And did not look back.

Bathsheba stood tall.

Crown on her head.

Shame behind her.

Her name restored.

Her story rewritten by the only One whose version had ever been true.

Elizabeth smiled.

Every prayer had been heard.

Every season of silence had been full of listening.

Not absence.

Attention.

The Woman at the Well laughed.

She would never thirst again.

The jar was cracked.

But it was full.

Priscilla spoke.

Her voice, clear.

Her voice, free.

The shawl was gone.

And the silence with it.

Mary Magdalene simply breathed.

Known.

Loved.

Called by name.

Home.

Jezebel stood without armor.

And was not afraid.

For the first time in her life.

She was not afraid.

Abigail set down her satchel.

Gently.

Completely.

For the very last time.

And straightened.

And breathed.

And smiled.

Twelve women.

Twelve stories.

One Kingdom.

One Father.

One welcome.

> *"But God, who is rich in mercy, because of His great love with which He loved us, even when we were dead in trespasses, made us alive together with Christ."* — Ephesians 2:4–5 (NKJV)

The Road Goes On

The music returned.

Louder than before.

Richer than before.

Fuller than before.

The gates behind them remained open.

Not to let them out.

But to let others in.

Because the bus was still running.

The Driver still on the road.

The invitations still going out.

The seats still waiting to be filled.

And somewhere, right now, another woman was holding a golden envelope.

Turning it over in her hands.

Reading her name.

And wondering if she was really expected.

She was.

She had always been.

> *"The Spirit and the bride say, 'Come!' And let him who hears say, 'Come!' And let him who thirsts come. Whoever desires, let him take the water of life freely."* — Revelation 22:17 (NKJV)

The road goes on.

The Kingdom waits.

The Driver knows the way.

And every woman who accepts His invitation is already known.

Already loved.

Already called by name.

The only question is whether she will get on the bus.

THE END

Acknowledgments: Those Who Traveled With Me

To God

This book was never my idea.
It was Yours. You gave it to me quietly, clearly, and with a certainty that left no room for argument. When I questioned whether I had heard You correctly, You faithfully sent confirmation through the people You placed in my life at exactly the right time.

You introduced me to twelve women I thought I already knew. Then You gently whispered, "Look closer." As I did, I realized I wasn't simply writing about them. I was finding pieces of myself in each one.

Their fears became familiar.
Their questions echoed my own.
Their struggles reflected seasons of my own life where Your grace was still transforming me.

Then You gave me a bus.
At first, I thought it was their journey.
But somewhere along the way, I realized it was mine too.
The bus became a reminder that life itself is a journey, and that every day You invite us to trust You a little more, surrender a little more, and become a little more like the people You created us to be.

You were already driving. All You asked was that I trust You enough to stay on board.
Thank You for trusting me with their stories.
Thank You for using their journeys to reveal more of my own.
Above all, thank You for reminding me that every road worth traveling begins and ends with You.

With all my love, gratitude, and praise.

To Mom and Dad (Helen & Tom)

You left when I needed you most.

For years, I learned how to carry that. How to build a life around the shape of your absence. But that is not where our story ended.

Somewhere in my adulthood, after I had already learned to live without you, you came back. Not completely. Not without the weight of everything that had passed between us. But enough.

Enough to sit in the same room. Enough to say the things that needed saying. Enough for me to see you not only as the parents who left, but as people, broken, human, and doing the best they could with what they had.

You are both gone now, and grief has a way of making everything more tender and more honest. I miss what we were able to rebuild, and I grieve what we never had the chance to finish.

Still, I carry you with me.

This book is for the leaving, the returning, the forgiveness, and the grace that met us along the journey. Thank you for giving me life. Our story wasn't perfect, but God's grace was present through it all, and for that, I will always be grateful.

To My Husband, Terrence L. Johnson

You never asked me to choose between the calling and the home. You gave me space to disappear into these pages and the love to come back to when I surfaced.

You prayed with me when I was stuck. You steadied me when I doubted. You believed in this book even in the moments I was not sure I did. That kind of love does not just support a dream. It makes the dream possible.

Thank you for being my rock, my sounding board, and my prayer partner. God knew exactly what He was doing when He gave me you.

To Family & Friends

You handed me your stories without knowing it. Every testimony I heard lives somewhere in these pages. Your courage made me brave enough to write.

You are the women who sat beside me when I was carrying things I could not name. You are the ones who said *keep writing* when I said *I don't know if this is any good.*

You are the reason this book exists. You know who you are.

To Dr. Linda Y. Cureton (Muse Technologies)

Thank you for believing in this story and in me. Your mentorship, wisdom, and encouragement helped transform these pages into the book they were meant to become. Your patience and thoughtful guidance challenged me to become a better writer while remaining true to the vision God entrusted to me. Thank you for sharing your expertise so generously and for helping me navigate the journey from manuscript to publication. I am deeply grateful for your partnership and for helping bring *Road to the Kingdom* to life.

To the Woman Holding This Book

I do not know your name. I do not know what you are carrying. I do not know how you found this book or who put it in your hands.

But I do not think it was an accident. You were invited before you ever opened the first page. The Driver has been expecting you.

Board the bus!

Tara A. Glover-Johnson

About the Author

Tara A. Glover-Johnson believes every person carries a story, and every story is worthy of redemption through God's amazing grace.

Her passion for faith, teaching, and encouraging others inspired her to write *Road to the Kingdom*, an allegorical novel that invites readers to examine the identities they have carried, the wounds they have hidden, and the extraordinary freedom that comes from surrendering both to the One who has known them all along.

Through the lives of twelve women drawn from Scripture, Tara explores timeless questions that every heart must eventually answer: *Who am I? What have I been carrying? And who might I become if I truly believed what God says about me?* Her hope is that readers will see themselves somewhere along the journey and discover that the road to healing begins not with perfection, but with an invitation to walk with the One who calls them by name.

Professionally, Tara is the Founder and Chief Executive Officer of TAJ Wanna Projects LLC, a licensed employment agency and workforce development firm, where she helps individuals, organizations, and communities grow through employment services, education, strategic partnerships, and career development. She also serves as an adjunct professor, where she teaches business, communications, project management, and leadership, encouraging students to pursue excellence with integrity and purpose.

Tara holds a Master of Business Administration from the University of Maryland University College (UMUC), a Bachelor of Arts in Communications from the College of New Rochelle, and is a certified Project Management Professional (PMP) and Certified Workforce Development Professional (CWDP).

Whether mentoring a student, leading an organization, speaking to an audience, or writing stories of hope and redemption, Tara's mission is the same: to help people see themselves through God's eyes rather than the labels the world has placed upon them.

Tara lives in Maryland, where she is a wife and a mother. She continues to write, teach, mentor, and encourage others to walk boldly in faith. She is a faithful member of From the Heart Church Ministries of Waldorf, where she continues to grow spiritually and serve alongside a community devoted to sharing the love of Jesus Christ.

Tara believes that every person is invited to walk with God. Her prayer is that when the Driver calls your name, you'll have the courage to answer, "Yes, Lord… I'm coming," and discover that the greatest journey you'll ever take is toward becoming the person God created you to be.

Made in United States
North Haven, CT
14 September 2026

18066002R00204